Jabberwocky's
Book

LOOKING GLASS SAGA

BOOK TWO

Jabberwocky's Book

TANYA LISLE

SCRAP PAPER ENTERTAINMENT

Copyright © 2015 by Tanya Lisle

ISBN-13: 978-1-988911-68-7

Scrap Paper Entertainment
www.scrappaperentertainment.com

Contents

CHAPTER 1

Haunted Dreams

THE FRIDGE TREES weren't going to save her. She thought about hiding inside one of them, hoping that they would bypass her entirely, but they would follow her everywhere. Those white eyes, all four of them, always figured out where she was and where she was going to be, no matter where she turned. With every attempt, they continued to hunt her down.

There was someone in the distance who was running as well. In the midst of all the trees there was a path. At the end of it, she could see a girl with brown hair and a lithe figure running with all her might to escape. No, not to escape. She was barely running at all. Instead, she seemed to dance through the trees, just out of reach as Alice continued to run.

The creature was after Alice, and Alice wasn't sure what she was trying to do anymore. Was she running from the beast or trying to catch this other girl? She turned hard into the trees, hoping to lose the creature long enough to figure it out, but still it followed.

Its long, ceramic white claws took a swipe at her, knocking several trees out of the way. No, escaping the creature came first.

She dropped down a hole that opened up out of nowhere. She knew this hole well. She still remembered the rabbit hole from the last time she'd fallen down it, as well as the strangeness that was inside. Down at the bottom, that brunette was looking up at her. She wore a uniform from Lucena Academy and a smile that Alice knew well.

Lori. Back and ready to see her again.

Before Alice's eyes, Lori turned into that creature, her eyes turning white and a second pair of them opening on her forehead. Her skin melted into that blackness and her fingers extended into those claws. And Alice fell into them.

Alice woke with a start, feeling like she'd just dropped down onto her bed from a very high place. That was happening a lot lately.

It took her a moment to realize that the darkness of her room wasn't, in fact, the creature come to swallow her whole again. Instead, it was just the regular old darkness that came from it being the middle of the night. There were no creatures in here to get her. Nothing of Wonderland or anything was coming for her.

Nothing except those purple eyes in the mirror, staring at her from a different world.

"Good morning, Alice," Cat said, almost purring through the mirror. "Sleep well?"

Alice glowered at the cat, his purple fur almost pressing against the mirror as he watched her from the other side of the room. He paced back and forth from the other side of the mirror, watching her and waiting for some response.

Instead, Alice went back to sleep. Or she pretended to, anyway. She pulled her covers over her and laid there, eyes hidden but still open. She reluctantly listened as Cat continued to speak. This trick never worked, but she didn't know what else to do.

"You should talk about your fears, dear girl. It isn't good to keep them trapped inside your mind like that. They will come for you more often if you do. If you would just let me out, I could provide you with some assistance."

She resisted the urge to yell at him. She knew better. She wouldn't be baited. She knew what he was trying to do.

"You have done a very bad thing, Alice," he continued. "There's something that you've released. The Queen was good enough to keep it hidden away, but you've set it free.

And you know how dangerous it is. Perhaps if you hadn't been so rash and quick to throw me away, I might have been able to help you contain it. Perhaps you wouldn't have to recapture it now."

Alice knew he was just trying to bait her. As he did every night. She wouldn't fall for it.

"You could let me out. Let me assist you. Or perhaps I won't. You benefit greatly if you request my assistance. You know that I know far more than you do on these matters."

She wanted to yell at him that he had never read the book. That he made her read it in exchange for peace. That he had been following her and wouldn't leave her alone because of something that he'd made her do. That releasing the creature wasn't her fault and that he didn't know any more about it than she did.

"Perhaps you could read it to me," he suggested. "That book does look so very lonely. You shouldn't leave them like that, all alone and unread. Especially one like that. It doesn't strike me as one that much likes being left all alone and ignored. It may have more tricks for you, Alice, and it will want you to pay attention to it sooner or later. Though I suppose you are getting quite good at ignoring your problems. Why, look at me. Me and whatever it was you let out. It will come for you, Alice."

Alice stayed still under the covers. She would stay still. She would be quiet.

"It might even come for that sister of yours. Ah, but you haven't even seen her, have you? She may have already been taken by the creature. That's what keeps you up so late, isn't it?" She could almost hear the curve of his lips into a wide grin as he spoke. "You don't know that it hasn't already found her. Perhaps that's why no one will tell you what happened to her and why she isn't here. Or perhaps they still worry for you. That you have gone mad again."

His laugh was as cruel as his grin, echoing off the walls of the room and threatening to wake the rest of the house. She pulled the covers tighter around her and prayed that no one else could hear him. He was an evil creature, that Cat, and she didn't want anything else to do with him. No matter how much he knew.

"You were always mad, Alice. Always."

Alice would have covered the mirrors if she thought her parents wouldn't consider it strange behaviour for her, and a sign that she might be slipping. She resisted the urge to throw a pillow at the mirror and make him go away. She wouldn't fall for his tricks. She was stronger than that and she would resist the urge to respond.

"You're not terribly fun," he said. "Perhaps I should see about that sister of yours. She left to escape the madness of this house, you know. Or maybe you do not. You do not know much, dear Alice. It is a shame. You would be more interesting if you did. But don't you worry. I shall return. Perhaps even with news of her. But you will only gain that if you let me through. Remember, now you will have to pay a cost to learn anything. As it always should be. We may be mad, but there are rules to *our* madness, Alice. Remember that."

Everything went very quiet after that. She didn't want to say anything in case he was still there waiting. She didn't even sit up to check. The silence stretched on until all she could hear was the beating of her heart in her chest and she remained very still. Waiting. Hoping that he really was gone.

She drifted off again, her sleep restless and full of creatures with four eyes following her.

$$\sim\!\!\sim\!\!\sim\!\!\sim$$

ALICE WOKE UP late that January morning, the Cat's words still floating through her mind as they usually did. He'd been following her since she'd returned home. He couldn't get through the mirror, he said. He was trapped there, though she had no idea why. He said she would have to let him back through.

She wasn't going to do that.

Now he appeared everywhere, following her wherever she went and badgering her. She did her best to not respond at all, but sometimes he surprised her. Still, she was glad her parents had yet to notice her strange behaviour. They were too distracted, though she didn't know why.

Everything had a layer of tension around it since she got back. Something had changed. They didn't tell her what, but it was something. Of course it was something.

Neither spoke much and, most notably, they did not speak of Lori. She had a feeling this all had to do with her sister. Lori did not come home from England for Christmas. Her father and her mother never so much as mentioned her name. When she tried to ask, she was very quickly and sharply cut off, making it clear that she was absolutely not supposed to mention her.

Alice was very good at taking the hint when she needed to and this was one of those times. What had happened with Lori, she didn't know. She probably didn't want to come home, too happy and having too much fun abroad, which upset her father. Her father was never happy when someone didn't do what he asked them to do.

Still, it was strange that she didn't even send word home. Alice wanted to hear from her, but she hadn't heard from her since part way through the summer. She was there when Alice was told she was allowed to go to school, but disappeared so soon after that. Where was she? And why wasn't she getting in touch?

Lori would have called her. She was so excited for Alice. Her father had let Alice go to Lucena Academy on the basis that she wasn't going to slip up anymore and it was time for her to learn to be a good, functioning member of this family. She needed to be smart enough to go to a school where she could snag a good husband who could take over the family business, or so her father told her, and Alice wasn't about to disappoint her father any further.

Lori would have gotten in touch with her somehow. She was the whole reason that Alice was allowed to go in the first place. She'd taught Alice the fine art of lying to get her father to let her stop taking the pills and lied to make her psychiatrists believe that she'd given up the delusion of Wonderland. It was all thanks to her.

She especially missed Lori at Mass on Christmas. Without her, it was dull. Her parents brought her every Sunday now and Alice didn't know when to sit or stand or when she was supposed to say what. Lori had been at her side to lighten the mood before as the priest went on about something she couldn't make out through the static filled speakers and actually made it fun.

She wouldn't have just left without leaving her a note.

Alice didn't trust it, but she knew better than to ask.

She got out of bed and went to her bathroom to splash a bit of water on her face to help her wake up. She didn't want to sleep any longer, those four white eyes still following her even as the sun leaked through her curtains into her room.

Alice even looked tired. She hadn't slept that well during this entire break. For a break, she'd been stressed like crazy. The end of the last semester with Cat and the book left her thinking, worried about whatever she'd let out and what happened. She worried she wouldn't be allowed to go back to school. She worried about where her sister had gone.

Sleep was not something that came easy to her anymore. But that was okay. It was nothing compared to her waking hours.

Water still streaming down her face, Alice checked the cupboard under the sink. It was a sacred place for her — a place to throw all the things she never wanted to see again.

There were bottles and bottles of little pills in all sorts of colours, every one Alice could name off the top of her head. Clozaril, Risperdal, Abify, Zyprexa, Seroquel, Geodon, and several others, all still at least half full with their menacing little pills. Since three months after she returned from Wonderland the first time, she'd been put on all of them at least once. She suffered through their side effects and was told all of them would make her realize none of it was real.

They were all wrong.

There were other things in here too. Little instruments that she was supposed to use to help her. The first book she'd written in about her time in Wonderland that was almost used to throw her into a hospital wing for the rest of her life. Lori managed to get it before her parents did and hid it away. As a present for getting a clean bill of mental health, she gave Alice the book and told her how close she came to being committed.

And sitting there guarded by all of this was the brown leather book. She got it back at the end of the semester, not sure whether she really wanted to keep it. On the one hand, it had caused so much trouble. It terrified her and she could still see that long claw coming out of the cover in the back of her mind, spearing a heart on the sharpened tip. On the other hand, she'd let something out of it and she would probably be the only one who could put it back. If she was even allowed to go back to school.

So far, her father said that he would let her return. They hadn't even heard about the time she spent in the doctor's after she fell in the lake. She wasn't about to let any of that go to waste.

"A shame, really. I know where it is and cannot retrieve it. You craft irony so elegantly."

Not that it was going to be easy to continue the charade for her parents.

She stood up and saw Wonderland in the mirror, as she often did when her mind wandered to it. She started to figure out that if she just didn't think about it, it wouldn't come for her. It was never quite the same place twice, and she wasn't sure that anyone on the other side really knew she was there.

But whenever Wonderland showed up, Cat was there as well, clawing at the mirror like Dinah used to do to her door, asking to be let in.

"Perhaps you could read me a page of it. It was so interesting the last time we read it. I would enjoy hearing more."

Alice found a towel and wiped her face. No matter where the mirror showed in Wonderland, he would always be there on the other side. And he would always want to talk.

"The worst of it is likely over, dear Alice. There can't be more left to release from the book. You have already released them all."

Alice left the washroom and went back into her bedroom, closing the door and staying away from her dresser mirror. He was following her and she knew how to avoid him. If she wanted to go back to school, she knew she would have to continue to not acknowledge Wonderland. Talking to a cat in the mirror would surely put her back on one of those pills again.

Instead, she went to sit at her desk and opened up her homework. She'd made a habit of doing a little every time Cat showed up as a way to get rid of him. When she drowned herself in the texts, her mind went back to the school and how much she wanted to make sure she was able to go back. She made herself remember the dorms and the classrooms, the classes and everything that was in the books.

Among those books was the novel assigned to read over the break: *The Hobbit*. It was about a small hobbit that was thrown into a surreal situation that he couldn't possibly deal with but, with help in the form of a ring he tricked out of a creature stupider than he was, he was getting his footing on the adventure. Alice didn't think it was quite fair the way he stole it. He may be a thief, but he didn't play fair by the rules of the game.

Bilbo was dear to her despite that. You couldn't always tell the truth to win. She knew that and, though it seemed irresponsible to put in a book, she found the story to be a lot truer in that area than anything else.

She had notes next to her, ready to write her report on the book when she was finished with it. It was going to be a bit of a long one and she was not looking forward to writing it all out by hand. She heard that they would be allowed computers next year and she was anxiously awaiting that. They taught her how to use computers at school and they were a lot easier on her wrists.

Gradually, she could feel Wonderland fade away. She kept reading until it was completely gone and she'd finished the book, the page next to her covered in notes. She glanced at the mirror, finding it only reflecting her room now, and got ready for the day.

It was noon when she finally left her room to venture out into the house. She always thought it was larger than it needed to be for four people. At least it meant a lot of days exploring with Lori when she was around. She missed her now that she was alone in the house again. Her parents were out, but Alice knew she was not alone. Not really.

She found herself at the door to Lori's room. It had been locked and abandoned since she left for England and Alice was curious about what was hidden behind it. She kept an ear out in the rest of the house, her eyes darting around to make sure she was alone. She looked up, checking the hallway cameras that her father had installed for security. The telltale red light was off, meaning he wasn't watching them. With one last look around, she took a step into the door and appeared on the other side.

Lori's room was much different from Alice's. Where Alice's room was sparse, filled with things appropriate for a little girl where necessary and lots of empty space for her to not hurt herself or distract herself with too much imagination, Lori's was filled with all sorts of things that lent themselves to all kinds of imaginings.

There were posters up on the walls of girl groups that Alice struggled to remember the names of. Littered on her bedside table were bits of scrap metal and gemstones next to pairs of pliers and other small tools. Lori made all of her own jewelry, though Alice was never allowed to wear much. Her items were so intricate and had a flair of fantasy about them that made her parents anxious that Alice could slip back into thoughts of Wonderland if she were exposed to them. Even at home, Lori was not allowed to wear them, though they were alone often enough that Alice saw most of them anyway. She always wanted one and Lori said she was working on something for her before she ran off to another country without so much as a good bye.

She also had the distinction of a television and a computer in her room — things Alice was forbidden from accessing most of the time. Talk of how they would rot her brain were the usual reasons, but Alice knew that they wanted to keep her from sinking into the worlds the screens opened up for her. Even if they weren't real.

Stranger, Alice found as she wandered through the old room, was the laptop on her desk. Whenever she left, Lori would bring up the password screen and close the lid, just in case someone came in. Now, it was open and off.

Beside it was her phone. Lori never went anywhere without her phone. She would carry it with her even around the house, texting with her friends from school over the break and sending them photos of the things she was working on. But here it was.

Lori would have called. Alice knew something funny was going on with her sister's disappearance and how her parents were acting about it, but she didn't know what to do about it.

Not yet.

CHAPTER 2

Time with the Family

"ALICE! ARE YOU awake yet?"

Her mother's voice rang out from downstairs. Alice turned to the door, already hearing the footsteps coming up. Her mother was supposed to be at work with her father, not home.

There was no time to be surprised and try to figure out how she hadn't heard her mother in the house earlier. Alice moved quickly, stepping away from Lori's room and appearing in her own by the door. She opened it to come face to face with her mother, trying to look like she wasn't just in a place she shouldn't be.

"I'm up," Alice said. "Morning."

"Almost afternoon," her mother said. She was a petite brunette that stood just a few inches taller than Alice. Alice couldn't remember a time she'd seen her mother without her face covered meticulously in makeup. Her hair today was tied back and she looked as tired as Alice felt. There was a bit of a smile on her face, something Alice hadn't seen at Christmas or much at all lately. "You shouldn't get in the habit of sleeping in so late. You've got school in a couple days. You've been doing so well that you don't want bad habits to settle in."

Alice nodded and said nothing.

"You've been doing so well. You wouldn't want to ruin it."

"Yes mom," Alice said, though the words felt strange. She'd been doing well. It meant that, despite their misgivings, they hadn't heard any word back of her misbehaving or otherwise acting strangely. She kept her grades up and she didn't raise anyone's alarm bells, or even their attention. That was the way her parents liked her. Normal as they could make her.

And, of course, there was also the threat. If she were to deviate from that — if she did ruin it — she was going to be right back to where she was before. Stuck here, in this house and in her room with the lock on the outside of the door.

She knew her place here. Not to worry.

She followed her mother downstairs and listened as she started chattering to Alice. This was what bonding was for them. Mom had a lot of pent up stress at work and Alice was her anxious audience, listening for news of the outside world and of anyone that wasn't in her immediate family or the people that passed through the house. Or the doctors.

Alice knew when to nod, when to laugh and when to look

indignant as her mother went on about office politics. She worked with her father at the bank, though Alice was never quite sure what either of her parents did there. Her father was in charge, though she thought that something like a bank might need more than one person in charge of it all. Mom was on a team of people who worked under him, all of whom would be at his beck and call should he need anything. She thought her mother was something like a super secretary, taking all of his calls and bossing people around that he couldn't be bothered to. At least, that's what it sounded like to her.

"But you've barely talked about school," her mother said, as if it were a sudden realization. "Are you liking it there?"

"Yes," Alice said, surprised that her mother was taking any interest in her at all. Both she and her father had been working most of the holiday, leaving Alice alone in the house with only her homework to keep her out of trouble. They hadn't even called Ms. Miller, her tutor, in to keep an eye on her. "I like it there."

Her mother waited expectantly, peeling a potato for the roast while Alice worked on the carrots. Alice shifted nervously under her gaze, her eyes returning down to the carrots and not sure what she was supposed to say. She liked it. She liked it and she absolutely could not talk about a large part of the things that happened.

"Have you made any new friends?" her mother pressed.

Alice nodded. "A few."

Her mother gave her a sarcastic smile. "Come on, Alice, I don't want to have to pry everything out of you. Tell me about school. We have all day."

Alice shifted nervously under her gaze. Since when was she ever interested in anything Alice did? She never asked when Alice came home crying from her appointments with the doctors or when the pills they gave her were making her head hurt. She never asked how her time with Ms. Miller went. Why did she care now?

She could still feel her mother's eyes on her and she knew that she wasn't going to be able to avoid this. "I'm friends with my roommate. Her name's Adrianna and she has a whole bunch of brothers." She looked up to her mother, who was actually listening and seemed to be paying attention, waiting for her to continue. "Most of them are a lot older than us, but Mike and Mark and, Matt are just a year ahead. They're nice."

"Are any of them cute?"

"What?"

Her mother let out a small laugh and nodded. "Keep going. Anyone else you meet so far?"

Alice kept going through and talked about all of the people she'd met that year, carefully choosing which facts she could share about them. Her mother wanted to know everything and Alice wasn't sure how much she really could say.

She watched everything, making sure that she didn't say any-thing that might hint at Wonderland and absolutely nothing about Cat. She tried not to say too much at all, but her mother kept pressing for details about them and stories about when they hung out, even though it was mostly just for studying.

Her mother also kept asking about the boys in a lot more detail. She wanted to know which ones were the cute ones and which ones Alice liked. Alice carefully dodged those questions as much as she could, eventually conceding that a few of the boys were cute just so that she could make her mother happy. The truth was that she was too busy worrying about Cat last semester to really think at all about any boys or anything else.

Maybe she should pretend that she was Sarah for a little while. Sarah would know how to have this conversation with her mother. Alice didn't think about which boys were cute or who she would want to spend more time with. Sarah was the one interested in that stuff.

She also asked for more information about Adrianna, which Alice was a lot more comfortable talking about. She liked Adrianna and wondered what she was doing this holiday season with all those brothers of hers. There was supposed to be one more that had already graduated and was now off at some university somewhere. She wondered how big their house must be to have that many kids in it.

"Maybe she'll invite you to stay one day," her mother suggested. They'd put the roast in and were cleaning up the mess they'd made of the kitchen. "That would be nice. I remember when I was your age, I went and stayed with one of my friends for a summer. We had so much fun and her brother and I... well, maybe don't do that." She laughed and Alice joined in, though she didn't know what was so funny.

"Oh, you're going to have fun, Alice," she said. "These are going to be good times for you."

Alice nodded, muttering something agreeable and wasn't sure where to go from here. She wasn't used to any of this and had no idea what her mother was looking for in this conversation. Maybe she'd be allowed to go up to her room soon to finish her book report.

"Is something wrong?" she asked.

Alice realized she probably looked like she felt for a moment and tried to correct it. It was already too late, though, and that look of concern was back on her mother's face. That look like she wanted to hear all about it all of a sudden. Alice wished she'd stop.

"It's just..." She knew her mother wouldn't stop pressing until she came up with something, so she had to think of something to be bothered by. She went with the first thing she could think of. "Why isn't Lori home?" she asked, her voice falling quiet. She knew it was a bad question, but somehow it was easier than telling her mother that she was uncomfortable about her interest in her life all of a sudden. "I thought she'd be back for Christmas and I haven't heard from her at all."

There was a mix of pity and fear on her mother's face. Maybe some regret. It moved and shifted, and her eyes looked so sad when Alice looked up into them, hoping for an answer. A moment of silence passed between them.

"It's okay," Alice said quickly, realizing staying silent would have been better than this. She knew what she was supposed to say. "She's in England."

"Yes," her mother said. "In England. It's best if you forget about her for now, Alice. Try not to bring her up again. You've been doing so well so far. We wouldn't want you to slip."

Alice felt an old sense of dread settle on her with those words. Doing so well. Wouldn't want you to slip. Lori was supposed to be like Wonderland, now? A thing that she never talked about, a thing that she pretended never existed?

Though the feelings hovered over her thoughts like a dark cloud, she pushed them back and righted herself, straightening up and putting a smile on her face that she didn't feel at all. "What about dessert?" she asked brightly. "What are we making to go with the roast for dessert?"

Her mother took the subject change and they went back to the cupboards, looking for something to make for after dinner. Out of the corner of her eye, Alice caught a shade of purple pass over the surface of a pot and back out of sight.

THEIR DINNER TURNED out well. Her father didn't arrive until almost eight for it, but he managed to get away from the office early enough that it wasn't too cold. Alice was grateful that her father hadn't taken any interest in her like her mother. He spent the meal talking to her mother about work and Alice ate in silence on her side of the table. She was thrown compliments like scraps that she graciously accepted and went back to keeping her head down. She couldn't handle two parents taking an interest in her in one day.

The pavlova that her and her mother whipped up at the end was even a hit and Alice was grateful that her father continued to ignore her for the most part, even when she went off to make tea for everyone. She stayed quiet throughout the dinner, letting her own thoughts marinate in her mind, that dark cloud of dread never quite settling.

Doing so well. Wouldn't want you to slip. She didn't like either of those being used to talk about Lori. She existed. There were photos of her around the house. More photos of her than there were of Alice. Or there had been before. Now that Alice looked around the dining room in small bursts while her parents weren't paying attention, she noticed that many of the photos of Lori were gone. They were replaced with just pictures of her parents on a vacation that Alice didn't remember them going on.

She wondered if the rest of the house would be like this too. She was used to not seeing herself in the photos. Alice was a disappointment that needed to be hidden away, but Lori was the favourite. She was able to convince her parents to let Alice leave the house and go to school. And she was the one allowed to attend the dinner parties hosted at the house. They wouldn't just push her away like she never existed at all.

She went back to her book report after dinner, finding Lori's pictures were indeed largely missing from the rest of the house. Alice tried not to think about it and threw herself into her notes about *The Hobbit*. It came easily to her, her mind desperately trying not to dwell on Lori. Her wrist was in pain an hour later when she finished.

With that done, she could now enjoy the rest of her vacation without having to think about her homework. All three days left of it. She needed to start packing soon.

Alice opted to start right away. There was no reason not to. She threw her school books in now that she was done with the homework, along with the clothes she would wear on the weekends. Toiletries came with her and she stopped in the bathroom amidst her collecting of things.

Underneath the sink, she pulled out the brown leather

book. She should leave it here. Maybe if she left it here, then she wouldn't have to go after whatever she released. Maybe if she ignored it, the creature would not come after her. It would come here, take the book from her room and go away to take hearts somewhere far away from here.

And then it would be Alice's fault.

Reluctantly, she picked up the book and threw it in her bag with everything else, packing it at the bottom of her school books. No one would notice it there and she could pass it off as an English book. She hoped no one would notice it.

The book drove people mad and the madness of the Queen of Hearts continued to consume her. According to Cat, she was ripping hearts out with her bare hands now. The book did that to her and, if Alice needed to read it to get rid of the creature, it might do it to her as well.

She threw in a couple of the pills that hid the book as well — only the ones with the least severe side effects. Maybe they would actually do something when she was going mad from reading the book. They might actually be worth something.

When she finished, the homework was the last thing to go in, packed neatly into a separate pouch to keep from getting ruined. She got ready for bed and went under the covers, grabbing a book on animals from the bookshelf with the intent to read it until she got tired. She really should ask for more books, since she'd already read all the ones on her shelf a few times over now.

She wanted to read *The Hobbit* again. It was a lot more fun to read than anything she had, but she knew better than to let her parents know that she was reading something like that for school. Fantasy was strictly off limits until recently, and if she showed too much interest, she worried that her parents would send her away.

Maybe she could convince them to get her some other novels. Something a bit more like real life so they weren't so nervous about it. Something more exciting than Jane Austen or Hemingway or any of the other books that she was only allowed to keep until she was done with them. Fiction that would not give her any of the ideas they were so worried about.

Besides, it wasn't the novels they needed to worry about.

A knock at her door a few hours later made her look up. She was already starting to drift off, having read this book often enough that she had pretty much memorised the contents as it was. She had taken a special interest in the section on felines again, but the book only repeated what she already knew.

"Come in," she said, sitting up in her bed to greet her visitor.

Her father walked in, still dressed in the suit he'd come home in and smelling faintly of cigarette. For a moment she was worried that he wanted to have a heart to heart like mom did, but he did not sit on her bed. Instead, he came up to the side and looked down at her, smiling beneath the moustache.

"Excellent dinner your mother and you prepared tonight."

"Thank you," she said, smiling.

"Your mother says that you're enjoying school," he continued. "Have you finished all your homework?"

Alice nodded. "And packed it," she said.

"How is your wrist?"

"It's a little sore from writing."

He laughed at that. "Only for the rest of the year," he assured her. "Next year, you'll be allowed to bring a computer to school for that. We'll find you a nice laptop when the time comes, hm?"

Alice smiled. She knew that this was supposed to be a generous gift from his tone, though she had barely used a computer in her life outside of computer classes. Everyone else in school seemed to already know quite a bit more about them than she did and she was fairly certain that she was the only one in her year that didn't have one of her own at home.

"We'll see what we can do for you come summer. If you keep cooking like that, though, you might just convince me to get you a particularly expensive one."

"If it's too much, I could always use Lori's old computer," Alice said. She regretted the words immediately. She didn't even know where they had come from, but she could see the darkness spread over her father's face, immediately and with a mix of anger with it. There was no sadness like when she mentioned it to her mother, only anger.

"You will get a new computer," he said firmly. "And you will only get one if you continue to not slip up. Just like you will only continue at that school so long as you do not slip up. Do you understand?"

"Yes father," she said. She met his eyes and kept from turning away until he was done staring her down. He left the room soon afterwards, the door closing louder than usual.

"I do not see why you ever left Wonderland," a voice said from the mirror. "The madness here is much more pleasant than the madness you've insisted on trapping yourself in there."

CHAPTER 3

Screams in the Light

UNLIKE THE REST of the students that milled about in the halls with their bags, Alice was glad to be back to school. She forgot entirely how difficult it was to keep herself together at home. At school, people weren't always watching and waiting for her to slip. They didn't assume she was about to. They didn't even know.

It was great to be back.

She got up to her room to find herself the first one there. A music player. That's what she should have asked for this Christmas. Adrianna had hers all last semester playing in the background until Alice barely noticed it, but the dorm sounded so quiet without it.

She started to unpack, making it almost all the way through putting her clothes away before Adrianna opened the door.

"Happy New Year!" Adrianna said brightly, dropping her bag by the door and greeting Alice with a hug.

"Happy New Year," Alice said, smiling widely. It was lonely here without anyone to talk to. It was strange that she would miss Adrianna this much over the holidays, but with her back, it made Alice realize how much she had gotten used to having someone else around. "How was your holiday?"

"Good!" she said, getting her bag and throwing it open. She spread her clothes across her bed and put her music on the speakers, the sound of soft pop music filling the room as Adrianna recounted her vacation. Her brothers were busy pulling pranks and they had her grandmother over. Her father and stepmother were only there with them for a day, but her eldest brother was back from school to spend the time with them.

Alice got out all of her homework and school books, arranging it all on her desk and nodding along, adding questions where she felt they were needed, but mostly staying quiet and letting her tell the story. Adrianna's family watched television specials and did all sorts of things together. Alice could almost imagine why it was so busy for some other people, but Adrianna still managed to get all of her homework done too.

"How was yours?" Adrianna asked as her tale wound down.

Alice sat on her bed and watched as Adrianna put her

things away, recounting very little. "Mass was kinda boring and my parents were working, so it was just me a lot."

"What about your sister?" Adrianna asked. "I thought you said you had a sister."

Alice hesitated to tell her about Lori. It was no use getting Adrianna worried as well about something that Alice could do nothing about. "She's not back from England," Alice said.

"Oh," Adrianna said. She sounded a little disappointed. "What about Wonderland? Did you go back?"

Her heart skipped a beat at the mention of Wonderland and Alice's eyes shot to the door to make sure it was closed. No, no one here was waiting for her to slip up like at home, but she said it just a little too loud.

Adrianna waited a moment before she looked back at Alice, expression concerned. Alice smiled and kept her voice down to a level that would definitely not be heard outside. "No, I'm not going back. I wasn't even supposed to go there in the first place. Do you know what my parents would do to me if they found out I'd been back there? I'd never be allowed to see the sun again!"

"But then what about Cat?" Adrianna asked, not lowering her voice at all. "Isn't he stuck over there now? Won't people notice that he's missing?"

"I don't care," Alice said, her eyes flashing to the mirrors in the room. "They were trying to kick him off campus anyway. I just made it easier for them. It's not like they could catch him anyway."

Adrianna giggled. "Evan told me about how they kept trying to corner him in the tree, but he kept somehow escaping and they couldn't figure it out. I didn't tell him about what he could do, but it was really funny."

Alice laughed too, imagining several people crowding around Cat's tree by the lake, all of them trying to shake him out, only to have Cat appear behind them. None of them stood a chance.

"If Evan really wants to talk to him again–"

"No, I think you're right," Adrianna said, still laughing. "I think he'd be happier if he never saw Cat again. It's going to be kind of weird without him following you around, though. I mean, not that it was *good* that he was following you! I just mean, he did that so much last semester that it might be kinda weird without anything weird happening this time. I mean–"

"It's okay," Alice said. "I'm hoping it's all over now. It would be nice to be normal. Well, except for the teleporting."

"You can still do that?"

Alice nodded, a broad smile across her face.

"Cool! Now all you need is to make sure the Jabberwocky doesn't come back, right?"

Alice's smile faltered. "Yeah," she said, trying to sound

upbeat. "So long as it doesn't come back, it should be a quiet semester." *And rest of my life*, she added to herself.

"I'm sure it won't be back again," Adrianna said, sounding far too confident about it. "You said it escaped into the woods. Why would it want to leave the woods? There's all sorts of things for animals in there, so it'll probably be happy there, right?"

Alice smiled, but she was unconvinced. She remembered it still. The claws, the white eyes following her. If it were happy staying deep in the woods and not coming out to feast on the hearts of her classmates, that would be great. Heck, even if it managed to leave the forest and go somewhere else entirely where the police could handle it, that would be awesome.

Not that the police would be able to deal with a creature that stole hearts and left the victim alive.

Not that Alice would be so lucky.

"And if not, you still have the book," Adrianna added. "If you need to take care of it, there's got to be something in the book about putting the creatures back in there, right?"

Alice nodded, looking back at her suitcase. It was closed and she left the book inside, not sure where to put it amidst everything else. She didn't want someone to come in and stumble on it looking for her copy of a text book or browsing through her closet.

There was no threat of a creature coming out of it anymore, so she could put it under her pillow or back between the mattresses. Or she could leave it in the suitcase where it wouldn't do anything. She could be safe from it, leaving it there along with the pills she brought in case she read it and it really did drive her mad.

"Alice?"

Alice snapped up to look at Adrianna. She realized she missed whatever Adrianna had been saying and shook her head. She tried to smile but it wouldn't come, the thoughts of what she might have to do still weighing heavily on her as much as Lori's disappearance. Instead, she looked up at Adrianna and met her eyes.

"Can you promise me something?" Alice asked.

Adrianna nodded, leaning in. "Of course."

"If... if it comes back. If something happens and I do have to do something about it and no one else on campus can do anything about it. If I have to read the book, can you keep an eye on me and tell me if I start to go crazy?"

"You aren't going to-"

"Please."

Adrianna smiled. "Of course I will. I promise. But you won't go crazy. I know you won't."

"It drove the Queen of Hearts crazy and now she's on a rampage trying to rip out everyone's hearts with her bare hands," Alice reminded her. "How can you be sure that I'm not going to do the same thing but out here it will actually end up killing people?"

"Because I read this," Adrianna said. She tossed the book back to Alice. It was the small notebook Adrianna had given her last semester that she had written out all of the crazy stuff that happened as a means to keep her from talking about it. "And because I know you. You aren't going to go crazy because the Queen was crazy to start with. You aren't. You'll be fine."

Alice smiled at her. "Thanks. But just in case?"

"I promise," Adrianna repeated, laughing. "But maybe you won't have to. I mean, you haven't seen it since, right? And if there was something attacking people out here, someone would have said something to our parents before we came back."

"How do you know?"

"I asked Evan and Joe," she said. "They said that if there were a bear or something in the woods, they would have sent a letter home to our parents and they'd be keeping everyone away from there until they got it under control."

"You didn't tell them about…" Alice waved the book to illustrate her point.

Adrianna shook her head. "You said to keep it a secret," she said.

"And you believe me?"

"Of course!" Adrianna said, smiling and getting to her feet. "Why wouldn't I? I've even met Cat and *seen* some of Wonderland. It looks like so much fun over there. And so pretty."

"It's not," Alice said, her smile returning.

"Can you take me one day?" she asked. "I won't tell anyone so no one else will ask, but it looks like so much fun over there. If we just avoid the Queen, it might be okay for a little while. We could have a picnic under one of those fridge trees, right? Then we'd come right back."

"It's not that easy," Alice said, still smiling. Adrianna, she could tell, genuinely wanted to go, but Alice wasn't going to subject her to that. "Trust me, it's really dangerous over there right now."

"Maybe when it's not so dangerous?"

"It's always dangerous," Alice said. "It's better here."

"Don't let Robert hear you say that," Adrianna said. "School is better than a magical place like Wonderland? He'd go crazy!"

Alice laughed and got up. "Speaking of," she said, anxious to not talk about Wonderland anymore, "we should go see if everyone else is here yet."

Adrianna followed her out and they went to knock on Sarah and Heather's door. Neither were there, but they weren't far off, having met up with Robert near the top of the stairs and were in the midst of catching up.

"Adrianna! Alice! About time you guys got back!" Sarah said, scooping them both up into a hug. "How long have you been here?"

"About an hour," Adrianna said. "We needed to unpack."

"Unpack?" Robert asked. "I just dropped my bag inside the door. Kevin's in there actually taking stuff out."

"At least he's not going to be up all night doing it," Sarah said. "I barely brought anything back."

"Except a giant make up kit," Heather said. "How do you plan on getting through all of that? There is no way all of those colours are going to look good on you."

"I'll think of something," Sarah said with a wink.

"You aren't even allowed to wear that much make up to class," Alice said, remembering a bit in the handbook about that.

"It's mostly just samples anyway," Sarah said, waving them off. "Mom brings home tons and asks what she thinks my friends will like, so she just sent me back with a bunch of stuff to check out and see what sort of stuff everyone would use. I'm probably going to give most of it away."

"So it's for market research," Heather said. She didn't sound impressed, but she wasn't condemning it either. "If you got anything for me, I'll take it off your hands."

Sarah smiled, her plans to offload it already working. "What were you guys doing on break? My family rented a lodge and we went skiing."

"Stayed home," Alice said, since Sarah was looking at her first. "It was quiet." She didn't want to elaborate much more than that.

"Me too," Adrianna said. "Grandma came by and my brothers were my brothers the whole time. But it was fun."

"I think we all had pretty quiet breaks," Heather said. "Snow and family, you know."

"Yeah, it was pretty dull this year," Robert said.

"Just be glad you didn't spend half of it on a plane," Kevin said, joining them from up the stairs. "Trust me, a vacation that consists of two twenty hour flights sucks. Next time, I hope my parents can come out here instead of making us all go there to visit the relatives."

There was some sympathy, though not much, for his plight. Instead, they made their way down the stairs, revealing who hadn't finished their homework and plans for the next semester. That didn't last long before the gossip started.

"So have you seen Cat at all?" Sarah asked Alice, sounding positively scandalous as she did so.

"No," Alice said.

"Aw, I bet he hasn't given up on you yet."

"Does he even go here?" she asked. "I bet he's gone off to

his own school or wherever he belongs this semester and he'll leave me alone."

"You're no fun."

"That guy seemed like kind of a jerk anyway," Heather said. "Didn't he get pissed off when you turned him down? Not the kind of guy I'd want to be around."

"Oh, she would have tamed him," Sarah said. "It would have been so romantic."

"Are you for real?" Kevin demanded, looking incredulously at her. "You cannot be serious."

Sarah laughed, waving it off as if she knew better than to listen to him.

Alice was glad to have them all back again. She missed having so many people she knew and could talk to so easily around. It was a lot better than her mother trying to ask her what her school life was like.

"Remind me to never let her set me up on a date," Kevin said. "She'd probably find me a serial killer."

"Hey, I would–"

The calm was shattered as a blood curdling scream rang through the large entry to the dorms. Every chattering voice stopped, everyone frozen by the sound of it as it rang through their bones. They closed their eyes and tried to cover their ears, but the chill ran through them all, freezing them in place.

Alice's mind cycled through images. Murder. Death. It

was like someone had actually reached into her heart and were actually trying to physically rip it out. She could almost see it as the screaming continued and she tried desperately to block out that sound.

What seemed like an hour was only a few seconds. The scream finally stopped and Alice, shaking, took a look around at the others. Some people were crying, others shaking as well. She felt her own face to find a few tears leaking out, not sure where they had come from but the feeling of something trying to pull out her heart lingered. She was shivering. Many people were.

A couple people were passed out on the ground, while some were curled up and looking dazed now that it was over. Confusion and fear spread through the room as the whispers began. Are you okay? Did you hear that? What was that?

Is everyone here?

That question echoed among them. No one knew quite who asked it, but the room went quiet again, people looking around and trying to count the heads. Who had screamed? Where were they? It sounded like someone was being killed, whoever it was. It was like they were being murdered in the middle of the foyer with the rest of them. Still, Alice could see no one missing.

"Everyone back to your dormitories," Miss Amanda told them loudly. "Go on, we're going to do a head count. Anyone who knows anything about this, head back to your dorms and we will be in soon to hear anything you know."

Alice and Adrianna headed back up the stairs with Heather and Sarah, all four of them looking shaken and haggard. Sarah had been on the ground, Heather now half carrying her up the stairs as she tried to keep her feet under her. Adrianna was having trouble stopping the tears from running down her face. Behind them, Kevin was carrying Robert, who was too out of it to move himself.

There were whispers as they shuffled into each of their rooms, Alice hearing many of them as she went in behind Adrianna. Someone was just killed, they thought. They all just heard a murder.

Alice shut the door behind them and went to get a roll of toilet paper out of the washroom for Adrianna to wipe her eyes and blow her nose with. She didn't know how to deal with a crying person, so she did what Lori always did for her when she was crying. She sat down next to Adrianna and put an arm around her shoulder and let her continue crying until she stopped.

After a few minutes, she started to calm down again, her eyes drying and able to form something coherent. "What was that?" she asked. "It was screaming, but it was so scary, like..."

"Like someone was being murdered?"

Adrianna nodded and blew her nose again, pulling back from Alice's arm. "What do you think it was?"

Alice's mind was already working. It had been since she first heard the scream. Screaming didn't reduce people to tears or leave them so shaken they needed help walking, that much she knew. If it was just screaming, no one would be on the ground or crying or so shaken like they were after it was over. That much just didn't make any sense. This was something different, something that no one else knew anything about.

Alice looked to her suitcase. "I think I need to start reading the book," she said, getting up and fishing it out of what was left in the bag. She left the pills at the bottom for now. Hopefully she wouldn't need them. "It was probably the Jabberwocky. It has to be."

She hesitated, holding the book in her hands again. She hadn't opened it since that night and she was scared it was going to bite her for holding it now. She didn't want to open it, but she knew she'd have to. She stared at it.

"Alice?" Adrianna asked, the terror back in her voice. Alice looked back, but Adrianna was pointing at the mirror beside her. In the reflection, a pair of purple eyes faded away, leaving a wide toothy grin behind for a long moment before it, too, vanished.

CHAPTER 4

Business as Usual

RUMOURS ABOUT THE scream echoed through-out Lucena Academy. There were no answers yet as to what caused it, only that everyone had indeed heard it and that no one was missing. There were no signs of foul play and no one had confessed to causing it yet. Adrianna's brothers were brought in for questioning, but they had a solid alibi in Travis, their older brother who was stopping two of them from pulling an unrelated prank, and the third being down in the foyer with everyone else when it happened.

People thought it was the seniors pulling a prank on the first years, but no one would confess to it. People started out thinking it was a prank, anyway. The lack of anyone willing to confess was weird, more because no one could figure out a plausible way of describing how they did it. Plenty of people were willing to take the credit, but no one could explain how they pulled it off.

Worse, there were stories of other people hearing similar things all over campus. It was never in a large group again and never identifiable by too many people, but there were rumours of it happening to random people throughout the first week of classes.

Some people thought this was all an elaborate hoax, but Alice listened intently for these stories now. It was always the same thing. It was a scream like murder and people were paralyzed by fear. No one knew what to do with themselves when it happened, only that they thought that they might die if they stayed there, but they couldn't bring themselves to move.

"I heard it was ghosts," Sarah said as they were gathered around a study table working on the homework after the first week back. Alice was determined to finish her homework every day right after class so that she could go hunting every evening after dinner, but no one else seemed to be as keen on it as she was.

"There's no such thing as ghosts," Kevin said. "Someone has to be setting this up. I mean, how hard could it be? Has anyone checked for speakers?"

"Actually, they did," Robert said. "I saw them going up in the attic."

"There's an attic?" Sarah asked. "Maybe we could go up there. If it's a ghost, then all we need to contact it is—"

Heather shook her head. "No, I've seen enough horror movies to see what happens there and I'm not doing it."

"Aw, come on," Sarah said. "Just one night, we sneak up in there after midnight and we try to contact the spirit. We might be able to put it to peace so it won't keep scaring everyone. We could be heroes!"

"The black person always dies in those movies and how many black people do you see here?"

Sarah looked around expectantly at everyone else.

"Oh no," Kevin said. "Without Heather, I become the token minority."

"It's not like this is *actually* a horror movie," Robert said. "It might be fun."

"Maybe we'll find a nice ghost," Adrianna offered.

"A nice ghost isn't going to scream like that."

"It might if it were trying to scare people away."

"So we're going to do it?"

"Do you even have anything to contact the dead?" Alice asked as she wrote in the last answer on her math homework.

"I can ask my parents to send a Ouija board," Sarah said. At Alice's blank look, she elaborated. "It's this board with a little pointer that you can use to contact the dead. You put your hands on it and it moves around on the board by getting pushed around by the ghost."

Alice looked at her blankly. "So someone pushes the pointer and everyone is supposed to pretend the ghost is doing it?"

"No, the ghost is the one that pushes it!"

Alice looked to Heather, who was shaking her head behind Sarah. Alice smiled. "I think I'll pass," she said, closing her book.

"While our roommates are off talking to ghosts, we can have a party and try to figure out who gets their stuff when they piss off the evil spirit and eventually get themselves cursed. It'll be fun. I know Sarah's got a ton of nice stuff that we can split."

"Anything for me in there?" Kevin asked.

"Hey!" Sarah said. She frowned, looking defeated. Adrianna looked a bit disappointed that she wasn't going to be talking to ghosts. Robert, on the other hand, just looked sad that he wasn't going to be spending more time with Sarah, though Alice doubted Sarah even noticed.

Alice slipped away as Sarah started talking about how ghosts were actually real, not really that curious about why she believed in them. Alice had much bigger problems than an imaginary ghost. She had to figure out how to trap the real

Jabberwocky to keep it from causing whatever it was doing to happen anymore.

Adrianna was up soon afterwards, Alice already at the desk and trying to figure her way through the book. She watched Alice flip through the book for information every night and helped her talk her way through it, which Alice was grateful for. "Why don't you just ask a teacher?" Adrianna asked.

Alice didn't even know where to start with it, the book more of a tome filled with too much information for her to absorb at once and most of it not even related to the Jabberwocky. She was still looking for a page on that, having trouble since some of the book was written upside down or needed a mirror to read. Some of it required she covered parts of the page before it made sense. Every page of the book was a different puzzle that made it hard to skim for the important bits. Slowly, though, it was getting easier. She wondered if the Queen went mad purely because of the layout of the book.

"Who would believe me?" Alice asked. She folded one of the pages into an accordion so that she could try to figure out what was supposed to be written on it. "I can't really tell anyone that I let something out of a magic book and it might be roaming the woods. 'Oh hey, Miss Bilamora! I kinda accidentally was forced to read a book by a cat from a place you've never heard of that let out this evil creature that I think is making the screams all over campus that seem to belong to no one and are causing absolutely no people to be missing.' I'm sure it will go over great."

"But she likes you!" Adrianna insisted. "She might be able to help."

"She'll think I'm working on some novel," Alice said. "Trust me, if you tell adults the truth about this stuff, they won't believe you and they'll try to lock you away. You don't want to do it."

Adrianna went quiet.

Nope, this was a page on birds. She went to the next one.

"What about someone else?" Adrianna suggested. "Maybe Joe or Travis could help. They aren't adults and they might—"

"Do you think they'd believe any of this?" Alice asked. She wasn't mad, but there was desperation in her voice. Adrianna didn't understand. No one would believe this. No one else could possibly believe any of this. "You are the only person I've ever met who would believe me about any of this stuff."

"Maybe all you have to do is show them. You could show them Wonderland. Show them that it's real."

"If my father found out that I've even been thinking about Wonderland, much less showing anyone—"

"But you have proof!"

Alice closed the book and stood up. "I need to go for a walk," she said. She took a step away from her desk and she was back by the auditorium, along the hallway with the window looking into the rooftop garden. It was dark out and the garden shimmered in the winter moonlight, but it was not quiet. Alice quickly realized she wasn't alone.

Down below, Alice could hear a few other people. The lines were unnatural and, even though she could barely hear them, she knew it was Old English. There were rehearsals still happening at this time of night, which meant she needed to find another place to pace and wander.

She walked towards the window and into the garden. It was beautiful out here, covered in a soft layer of untouched snow. It could have been another world entirely. The leaves of the trees were half ice and the light, fluffy snow was tarnished only by Alice's socked feet.

Alice very quickly realized why this was a bad place for her late night walk. It was a shame, really, that the night wasn't quite as late as she thought it was.

Thankfully, the library was closed at this time, which meant that she was alone to wander through the stacks and stacks of books. Her feet were not too wet from standing in the snow in her socks, but she moved quickly anyway in an effort to keep them warm. Already, she could feel some of the frustration melting away a bit as she paced through the smell of the old books and the dimly lit, narrow halls of shelves.

Just go get help. Sure, it was that easy for them. They

didn't know what she knew and they certainly didn't know what the consequences of those actions were if she tried. So much as mentioning Wonderland meant she was given pills and counselling sessions and locked away in her room where no one would hear her pounding on the door.

Alice knew what happened to little girls who told people that there was some creature in the halls chasing after them. She wasn't going to risk her freedom over a question. She wasn't going to be sent away like Lori probably had been for whatever she had done. She was going to figure this out on her own and she wasn't about to let anyone lock her up.

Everyone else could run to the teachers with their problems. Their problems were people and people were things that teachers could handle. Alice's problems involved Wonderland bleeding over into the school and she would have to deal with them herself. If she didn't, her father would hear of it and that could not happen.

She wished Lori were here. She was the one who knew what to do to make the doctors stop. She knew how to get Alice to the school. She wouldn't be saying something like tell a teacher. Lori would know what to do.

Wherever she was. After she figured out this Jabberwocky thing — right afterwards — she would figure out where Lori went and how to get her back.

Alice knew she shouldn't be mad at Adrianna. She didn't

know. She got to go home to a family full of brothers who would pull the attention off of anything she did if there was something wrong. And Adrianna was trying her best to help. She was just in very far over her head and there was nothing that Alice could reasonably expect her to do about it.

It was still frustrating that she didn't get it. There was probably no way for her to get it in the end. Alice knew that she would have to accept that. She was helping as best she could.

Alice saw something move in the library with her and ducked down behind one of the shelves. She didn't see much of it, only a glimpse of something moving and it was gone again. Cautiously, she stepped back around the shelf and slipped behind it. Whatever it was, it was no longer there when she looked again. She saw something moving a few shelves down, furry and slinking through the library.

What was she doing? This thing — this creature she'd let out — was huge and dangerous. It stole hearts out of people's chests. It was responsible for the place that was now Wonderland and the madness of the Queen of Hearts. Why was she chasing it? She didn't know how she was going to catch it. She didn't know how she was going to keep it caught.

It wasn't in here with her. She was in here with it. This time, the screaming would be her own and she was going to lose her heart. Someone would find her here with a hole in her chest.

The panic raced through her as she tried to think of somewhere to run to. Anywhere. Back to the dorms. Yes, she would go back to the dorms. The dorms would be a safe place for her. She started to move from her spot when that brown fur moved out of the corner of her eye.

Alice tried to take that first step to get out of there, but her head turned to look.

Bad idea.

Worse was the sound that came out of it, once again sending Alice down into the pits of her mind. The scream scratched at her bones, trying to peel them clean of her flesh. She couldn't even bring herself to cover her ears or close her eyes as her mind reeled in the panic and the terror as the scream continued.

All the pain, the horrible things that existed in the back of her mind shot to the forefront. The memory of hearts being torn out and the beating of that room as every trapped heart in Wonderland beat at once around her. She couldn't handle it all at once. Now, the hearts were floating in blood and she could see the faces, all devoid of life, all dead and still moving about with their hearts beating all around her.

And that creature, dark and with those horrible white eyes and porcelain claws crawling closer and closer to her. She couldn't move. The claws were covered with blood and they were coming for her, ready to strike and take her heart as well.

She wanted to run away. She needed to get away from all of this. She was trapped in here with this thing and there was nothing she could do about it. Why did she want to catch it? It was going to kill her or take her heart and send her back out. Her heart would join the others, beating forever over and over in that room, constantly drumming until it finally stopped.

When the scream finally ended, her need to run was the only thing that saved her. Her knees buckled and she collapsed into a brightly lit room, shivering on the floor and trying desperately to claw the images out of her mind. Her voice was gone and she couldn't make a single scream, nor could she hear anything but those other screams echoing in her mind. She was stuck, trapped in there and there was no getting out.

Something touched her shoulder and she let out a yelp, her body able to move again as she leaped back. She was away from it. She ran away. This was her dorm room. She she was back with Adrianna, who approached Alice like she were a wounded animal. Slowly, she sat down on the floor in front of her.

"Alice?" she asked, her voice soft and her hand hesitating in front of her. She made no sudden movements and waited for a sign from Alice.

The adrenaline was still pumping through her veins, keeping her from feeling calm, though she tried. Adrianna started miming deep breaths and Alice tried to follow along.

In and out. In. Out. In. Out. Her breathing slowed, though she couldn't stop shaking.

Finally, Adrianna reached over and helped Alice to sit, staying next to her and leaning against her bed.

"I'm okay," Alice said eventually. "I'm... I'm going to be okay. I'm sorry."

Adrianna looked relieved. "What happened?" she asked, taking one of Alice's still trembling hands.

"I think I found it," Alice said, her eyes fixed on the floor. "In the library. It was the Jabberwocky. I don't know if I can do this."

"It's okay," Adrianna said. "Maybe you don't have to. Maybe someone else will."

Alice didn't like that answer.

"And in case they don't," Adrianna added quickly, "I'll help. We can figure it out together. You don't have to do it all on your own this time."

Alice smiled. Help. It was a really nice sentiment, but she had no idea what Adrianna would do to help. Still, in this moment, she wanted nothing more than to believe that someone would be able to help her.

CHAPTER 5

Ghost Charms

"BUT VALENTINE'S IS coming up!" Sarah protested. "You can't *not* have a date on Valentine's!"

"Sarah, *lay off*," Heather said, putting her hand on her shoulder and pulling her away from Alice. "It's two weeks and Alice can do whatever she wants for Valentine's. Including not celebrating."

Alice stared wide eyed at Sarah, not sure where her reaction had come from. All Alice said was that she didn't really do anything to celebrate Valentine's and she wasn't planning on finding someone to celebrate with. She didn't even know that much about Valentine's except that was when her parents usually went out. Ms. Miller gave her a history lesson on the day once and she'd seen all of the red and pink everywhere, but she didn't really know much about the dating part.

Alice didn't know what people did on a date but, looking at Sarah, she thought it best not to ask her. She knew that you were supposed to go out and have dinner or something, but she didn't see how that was much different from having lunch with everyone here. First years weren't even allowed to leave the campus for food or some kind of a show. There was nothing that she could think of that you could do here that constituted a date.

Sarah looked on with such disbelief that Alice felt a little bad for her. "Sorry," Alice said. "Maybe next year?"

Sarah considered this and Heather took her hand off her shoulder. A smile split across her face. "Next year, if you don't find someone on your own, can I set you up?" she asked, a twinkle in her eye, possibilities already going through her mind.

"Do I have to put you on a leash?" Heather snapped at her.

"Okay, I guess?" Alice said. She didn't know what that meant, but it was a whole year away. She could think of a way out of this whole thing by then. That, or she could ask someone to spend the day with her and they could pretend to date to satisfy Sarah. Or maybe she could get an actual date, if she could figure out what you did on one of those.

Sarah smiled and clapped her hands. "Perfect! In a year, we'll talk. I'll find you someone perfect!"

Heather shook her head as Sarah wandered off. "You have no idea what you got yourself into. She is never going to forget that. She would probably break you up with whoever you're with next year just so she can play matchmaker."

"I'm sure it'll be fine," Alice said. "She'll forget."

"No, she won't," Heather said. "She'll remember. When it comes to this, she will always remember. She's like Venus or Aphrodite or something. I swear to God, I need to put a leash on her to keep her from meddling in everyone's lives."

"She's just trying to help."

"Oh, I know. She doesn't think she's doing anything wrong, but there's a reason I went and got a date for the dance weeks in advance and didn't tell anyone, know what I'm saying?"

Alice smiled and said nothing. It didn't need to be said. While Heather was more annoyed with her than anything, Alice thought it was sweet that she was trying, albeit forcefully, to make people happy.

It was a much better use of her time than trying to hunt down a monster.

"Why does Sarah look so happy?" Kevin asked as he joined them. "It's just like someone handed her a mysterious new transfer student that she's about to make over into something."

"Or Alice agreed to let her play matchmaker."

"Alice," Kevin said, pitying her.

"It's not until next year!" Alice said. "I'm sure she'll forget all about it by then."

"Or she'll start coming up with a list now," Heather said. "Oh Alice. So young. So naïve."

Alice laughed. She needed this. It was good to hang out with her friends now and then. Adrianna noticed that she was getting squirrelly after reading the book so religiously that she had to beg Alice to take a break from it.

Adrianna was busy these days. She joined the choir and that left Alice on her own a few afternoons a week for a couple hours before dinner. That, of course, meant that Alice had plenty of time without her designated watcher there making sure she socialized so she didn't go crazy. That, or she'd catch up on sleep, since she spent so much time wandering the halls late at night.

"If I were you, I'd throw myself to the ghost now," Heather said. "It'll be way less painful."

"God, that ghost," Kevin said. "Can you believe there are *still* stories? Apparently one of the guys a year ahead of us just heard it again last week."

"Really? Where?"

"Out by the forest. They really need to figure out what's causing all this. Everyone talking about how there's a ghost haunting the campus is just stupid."

"Who's to say that there isn't really a ghost out there, though?" one of three possible voices said behind them. Two identical and very familiar faces were there, smiling and looking like they were ready to make a sale. She recognized Mark by his voice, but wasn't sure which of the other two was with him just yet.

"We don't want any," Kevin said quickly.

"Aw, you haven't even heard the deal yet," the other one said. "We have a way to scare the ghost off."

"Wasn't one of your roommates the one that saw the ghost the last time?" Kevin asked.

"Yeah," the lighter voiced one said. "Trevor is never going to be the same again after that. Said the scream made him remember all the terrible things in his life or something like that. He'll be fine, though."

"Despite never being the same again," Heather said.

"Precisely! And if you don't want to end up like Trevor, who is still cowering in his room after what happened, we have a little something that should be of some use to you!"

The higher pitched one held up a few lumpy metal coins that had been stamped with a strange symbol Alice didn't recognize dangling on the end of black cord. There were lines and curves that she thought she recognized as Mesopotamian from one of her books at home, but what it was supposed to be, she didn't really know.

What did catch her eye was the lack of a mole on his palm as he held them up.

"Made from real silver and guaranteed to keep the ghosts

away," he said with a flourish. "No one who's been wearing one of these has been able to so much as find the ghost, much less have it sneak up on him in the middle of the night. And, since you're Addie's friends, we're willing to part with them at a bit of a discount."

Kevin rolled his eyes at the pitch, sitting back with his arms crossed as Heather leaned in to get a closer look. The one Alice now knew to be Mike gave her one to look at a bit more closely. She turned it over in her hands politely, not sure what she was supposed to do with it.

"Come on, Heather," Kevin said. "You can't really—"

"Let the lady make up her own mind," Mark said, cutting him off with a sly, salesman smile to Heather. She was transfixed on the necklace.

"What's the symbol?" Heather asked.

"Sumerian," Mike told her. "It was put on the graves of kings to ward off evil spirits. You'll have no better protection. If it keeps them away from kings, then I'm sure you'll be plenty safe. You trust me, don't you?" he asked with a charming smile.

That almost broke the spell they had over her. At the dance at the end of last semester, she spent it with Matt, the one brother not here that asked her to help cover for them in exchange for the date, which Heather was more than happy to do. She had a bit of a mischievous streak, though she was unable to act on it herself. Something about expectations of her parents and not wanting to get in trouble, so she agreed on the condition they didn't switch her all night.

She was never quite sure if they did.

"But Mike, didn't she go to the dance with Matt?" Alice asked, completely innocently.

Heather looked at her, then back to Mike who was not faltering. Mark behind him looked a little flustered, but Mike didn't miss a beat in the midst of the sale. "Just because my brother is a better date doesn't mean you can't trust me," he said. "I wouldn't want to see any harm come to you either."

Kevin smacked himself on the forehead as Heather's fight completely went out of her. From the look of it, Kevin wasn't going to try and even fight it anymore, but he didn't look all that amused that Heather was buying anything from them. She was even picking out a second one, presumably for Sarah.

Mark swept in behind Alice and smiled a tight smile. "A word?" he asked, nodding off to the side.

Alice followed him a few steps over, still in sight of the transaction, though far enough away that she wasn't able to interfere anymore. She smiled innocently at him.

"What was that about?" Mark asked.

"What was what about?"

"Oh come on, you can't play innocent with me," he said. "We have been playing this game a lot longer than you have."

"It was just an honest question," Alice said. "Unless you were trying to trick one of my friends into buying some coins on a string that were printed in Mesopotamian and not Sumerian. Do you really know what those symbols mean?"

"What do you want?" he asked, smiling a little. He knew that Alice had him.

Alice's mind worked quickly and her smile did not falter. "I want to know what happened to Trevor," she said. "Kevin said he actually saw something. What did he see?"

"Oh, that?" Mark looked almost bored. "He says that it was the ghost, but there was this dark huge thing in the woods. It's probably just a bear. He heard the scream and looked back and saw this thing in the woods running away. The school's already set something out into the woods to catch it. Bear trackers or something."

"It's a bear?" Alice asked. "Weren't you the one that was here when that thing screamed on the first day? Do you really think that was a bear?"

"I think that was someone a lot faster than we were," Mark said. "A good speaker system and a random blood curdling scream. It was a great prank and they cleaned it up really fast. I'm betting someone has access to the attic from their dorm room so they were able to get it out fast. Damn jealous. I wish we'd thought about that."

"But what about the rest of the people who say they've heard it?" Alice demanded. "It doesn't add up."

"Some of them are lying," Mark told her. "It's an easy way to get out of class. Some people thought they heard something and it freaked them out so much that they thought it was also this thing. And then Trevor saw something and got so freaked out about a bear that he thought it was the ghost. It's just rumours, Alice. Nothing's actually there. Come on, I expect Adrianna and your friends to fall for this stuff, but not you too."

Alice didn't have a rebuttal to that one. She knew it wasn't just a bear or anything else they might come up with, but she had some idea of where it was now. She could work with that much.

"Mark my words," he said. "When all this rain clears up, someone will say that this whole thing was a bear in the forest that probably got into the school and started wreaking a little bit of havoc. People will feel stupid about thinking it was some ghost and we'll get away with a nice profit. Well, so long as no one ruins it for us."

Mark smiled, squeezing her shoulder a little too tightly before he winked and went over to rejoin his brother. Mike kissed Heather's hand for a lovely transaction and in hopes that, if she didn't hook up with Matt again, then she might give him a chance. Heather looked sufficiently flattered, while Kevin shook his head as they left.

"I cannot believe you fell for that," Kevin said as Alice returned. "Those things don't really work, you know. It's probably not even real silver."

Heather wasn't even listening, fastening the charm around her neck and handing one to Alice. "Here," she said. "He gave me a great deal on three of them. I'm sure they'll just give one to Adrianna, though. I mean, she's their sister."

"So you believe in the ghost?" Kevin asked. "You really believe there's a ghost that suddenly appeared on campus this semester and did nothing at all ever before. And that all it does is scream? It doesn't move things around and it doesn't kill people, it just screams?"

"No one's died yet," Heather said, Alice putting the necklace on as Heather looked on expectantly. "With these sorts of things, you never know when it might escalate. It could only be a matter of time before something comes up and snaps in it, and then it starts wanting blood. Or maybe someone to join it in the afterlife."

"It's a *ghost*!" Kevin said. "Ghosts aren't real! Alice, help me out here."

"I need to work on that essay for Socials," Alice said quickly, picking up her bag. "Thanks, Heather."

Heather gave Kevin a *See, she agrees with me,* look and Alice nodded to Kevin and Heather before she headed back up the stairs. Alice smiled the whole way up, glad both to have gotten out of that particular conversation with the two of them and that she now had a bit of a lead.

Homework first. Once Adrianna came back, she could start on her research again.

CHAPTER 6

Study Break

ADRIANNA WAS LATE getting back this evening, but that didn't stop Alice from diving into the book. Without her there, she could prepare for the session by marking the pages with post-it notes so she knew what to look up when she got back.

There were parts of the book that she was getting used to. There were only really five different types of pages and she had now mastered how to read all of them, how to turn the book or use a mirror or fold the page in order to read what was written on it. It wasn't really split up into sections either, sometimes an article ending on one page and continuing a few pages later, which made for a difficult time to figure out anything.

Still, she found a few pages that were left untouched. One of them was the Jabberwocky's, which was missing the illustration from the top of it. It said a lot of things that Alice didn't understand and there was no dictionary that would tell her what "frumious" was supposed to mean, but she got the idea of what sort of thing she was up against. It was a creature with claws and teeth that she should avoid and probably something that knew how to change size, if the previous experience with it in the library was any indication.

If it was from Wonderland, all it would need was a little mushroom. Or a bottle of liquid. Or cake. Heck, if it ate *anything* it might grow or shrink or have its middle wish granted or be given the ability to travel across the forest with a single step. It came from a book from Wonderland, so it could probably do everything that Wonderland could do.

She stopped to stare at the page to remind herself just what she was up against. It was not something she would be taking lightly and she knew a few things she was going to try to do to help combat it already. Like borrowing Adrianna's music and playing it so loudly that she couldn't hear the screaming. So far it hadn't attacked Adrianna, but she didn't know how long that would last.

She went to another page, one she marked now with a Post-it note. There were pages in the book dedicated to things she could say and do to keep the creatures from attacking and for catching them. She went through to find all the pages that had the small star somewhere in the margins, hoping for something she could use. Something to wrangle and catch monsters, to help defeat them. Alice didn't know if she'd be able to defeat anything, but maybe she could hold it off and catch it long enough to figure out what to do with it.

"Studying all alone, child?"

Alice looked around to find a pair of violet eyes staring back at her from the mirror she kept next to her to translate the pages. She saw him now and then, now always looking out from the same empty field instead of various spots around Wonderland, but it had been a while since he spoke to her. Maybe he didn't want Adrianna around. Maybe he knew not to talk when anyone was around at all. She didn't know why he decided to speak now.

"What do you want, Cat?" she snapped at him, still working through the pages, looking for the symbol to mark out.

"Oh, so she can speak!" he said, sounding positively delighted as he nestled against the edges of the mirror. "I worried another cat had been here to take the important things that cats are supposed to take. And after so much protesting you are finally reading the book! A shame you keep trying to make me read it as well. So clever, Alice, trying to drive me mad along with you."

"I never asked you to spy on me," she said. "That's your choice, not mine."

"Ah, but I wouldn't be so concerned with you if you

were the only one to be concerned with. Perhaps I could be bothering someone else. Perhaps that Jabberwocky would be catching my attention instead. And I could be worrying about that instead of you."

"You'd never take on the Jabberwocky," she said. "I've seen it and you are not going to take that thing on."

"You underestimate me, dear Alice," he said. "A cat's bravery is equal to the reward at the end. Perhaps a little less so."

"I'm not letting you out of Wonderland," Alice told him. "You are staying on that side of the mirror and once the Jabberwocky is back in Wonderland, then I hope I never have to see Wonderland again."

"You wound us so, Alice," Cat said, though she could not hear a hint of sincerity in his voice. She never looked at the mirror, but she was almost certain he tried to look as taken aback as he could manage. "We wanted nothing more than to entertain you when you came here. You were such a delight! Perhaps if you hadn't been so terribly rude, you might have enjoyed our company more, but you understand that one cannot tolerate such rudeness."

"I'm still not letting you out," Alice said, putting a blue note on the marked page. That would be good enough for now. One of these had to have something on them about silencing and luring the creatures in the book. If she could figure out how to do that, then she could stand a chance against it. Once she figured that out, she could hopefully find something about trapping them as well. If not, then maybe she would just lure it right into Wonderland and be done with it.

"I wouldn't be opposed to a switch, Alice dear," Cat said, trying to sound as sweet. Alice could almost hear daggers in his voice, and the threat that he wasn't one to be ignored or crossed. "Over here, you haven't released anything. Wonderland has no strange things that go bump in the night. There is no night at all, unless you want those imbecilic men with swords at the castle in servitude to the Queen of Hearts. But I don't think they would be of much help to anyone, would they?"

"More helpful than you are."

"I am insulted!"

"Why do you even want out, anyway?" Alice demanded, picking up the mirror. "All you have to do is avoid the Queen and you're fine. And I know how hard you are to catch. You don't have to worry about anything but maybe moving out of the sunny spot on the grass every few hours. You certainly don't need to spend so much time annoying me."

"But the Mad Hatter has been quite annoying of late. Far more than I." Cat floated lazily to the other side of the mirror, now upside down and looking like he was lying on the top curve. "He seems to think that he knows where that dratted Hare is and he won't stop *insisting* that I assist in rescuing him. He seems to think I should care as much as he."

"That's not my problem," Alice said. "You know how to not be found. Don't let him find you. I have bigger problems."

"Yes, fixing your own mistakes and putting away a monster you released."

"That you *made* me release."

"I merely gave you a suggestion. A suggestion is not enough to condemn a person."

"It is when you do it like that!" Alice slammed the mirror back onto the desk face down. She still remembered him hunting her down, him threatening Adrianna and her if she didn't do what he wanted. She shouldn't be indulging him in conversshe waation at all. "If you think after you did all that, that I'm going to let you out of Wonderland…"

"Not even to deal with this pesky Jabberwocky for you?" Cat appeared in the wardrobe mirror, clicking his tongue a few times and shaking his head. "So much spirit, Alice. You think that you are the only one who is suffering. I have had to listen to the Hatter go on and on about how the Hare got himself caught and how much he needs a distraction. He seems to be coming to his senses, which is quite a terrible thing for someone to do. He hasn't even faced the Queen yet and I dare say he's starting to make as much sense as the people on your side."

"Still not my problem," Alice said. She flipped back to the first blue note in the book and started to fold the page. She would only read the heading and figure out which pages might be helpful when Adrianna got back.

"Wonderland will always be your problem, Alice." The Cheshire Cat didn't sound playful anymore, though Alice resisted the urge to see why the stainless steel lamp on her desk had turned purple. "When Wonderland chooses someone to share in the madness, it does not let go just because you want it to. You're one of us. You always will be. And that will never not be the case."

"Is that Cat?"

Alice looked back, Adrianna dropping her things in the doorway and rushing over to Alice's side, staring into the lamp. She yelped and took a step back.

"That's Cat," Alice said, going to the next blue note. She spun the book in front of her to make out the winding text on the page.

"That doesn't look like Cat."

"Not very bright, that one," Cat said, amused as he moved out of the lamp and into the wardrobe mirror.

"That's what he really looks like," Alice said.

At least Adrianna seemed to be taking this well. Most people would be worried that there was someone going crazy in the room if there was a talking purple cat in a mirror that now showed a sunny field full of decapitated flowers. He fluttered about the mirror and seemed not at all concerned about the strangeness or even that Adrianna was here.

Adrianna went closer to the mirror, her eyes crawling over Cat and the scene behind him. Tentatively, she knelt down and tried to touch him, the glass stopping her fingers from going through as Cat ignored her.

"He's a cat," she said.

"Yep."

"You should be careful of this one," Cat said, jumping back into the mirror on Alice's desk as she picked it up again. "She is much brighter than she appears."

"Would you go away and stop insulting my friends?"

"Remember my words, Alice."

Cat disappeared from the mirror and took Wonderland with him. "Finally," Alice muttered, putting the mirror up to the next page and trying to read what it was about. No, this was about making it easy to get close to the creatures once they were already found. She didn't really want to get any closer than she had to. Where was something to make it go back to Wonderland so she could forget this whole thing?

"Has he been there the whole time?" Adrianna asked as Alice went to the next page she marked out.

"Just since I started today," Alice said, not looking up

from the pages. "He's been watching every time I open the book, though. I think, anyway."

"I've seen his eyes sometimes," Adrianna confessed. "Just when you're reading. But I wasn't sure if they were him because the mirrors all get kind of weird whenever you read."

Alice didn't say anything to that. She knew that every time she opened the book, Wonderland appeared in bits reflected around the room. She didn't know how to make it stop and an apology for doing it didn't seem like it was enough. She worried that they would become portals one day and someone other than her would fall through.

She needed to figure out how to put the Jabberwocky back in Wonderland. Once she managed that, she might not even ever think of Wonderland again. She could get rid of the book after that and it would be over.

"He can't get out," Alice told her, hoping it would help. "He's stuck in Wonderland because I won't let him come back."

"You can do that?"

"Apparently." Alice smiled at that, the thought making her happy though she didn't know how it worked. "Oh, hey, this might be useful!"

She looked in the reflection to find that this page had a method to make everything go quiet in an area. It was supposed to be used on herself, so that she could better sneak up on other creatures, but she could also use it on someone else. There were more words that she would have to swap in and out if she were going to make it specific to other creatures, but it would be perfect. If she could keep it from screaming, she could actually stand a chance.

"Can I see?" Adrianna asked, Alice moving to the side to let her look in the mirror at the translation. Adrianna leant down to get a better look, but Alice watched as her eyes glazed over trying to read it. It wasn't a glassy-eyed expression so much as a literal layer of gloss over her eyes. She stumbled a step backwards, clutching at her head with one hand and Alice's chair with the other, laughing to herself.

"Sorry," she said, shaking her head and righting herself. "That was weird."

"Are you alright?" Alice asked, watching her face carefully as she continued to shake whatever had come over her off. The high gloss finish on her eyes faded away and she seemed alright.

Adrianna laughed to herself, looking a little embarrassed. "I'm fine," she said. "I don't think I'm supposed to read it like you are, Alice. I don't think it likes me. It sounded a little mad."

"Sounded mad?" Alice asked. She looked between the book and Adrianna, who was shaking her head and didn't think there was anything strange about it.

"Not sounded," Adrianna said, heading back to sit on her own bed, nursing her head. "It's just... I don't think it wants me reading it. It's probably nothing. I'm okay, really," she added when Alice didn't look convinced. "You said you found something. Have you found enough to catch it yet?"

Alice hesitated, looking over Adrianna. She looked fine. She went back to the book, flipping back between the pages. She told Adrianna about what she found so far, Adrianna nodding and trying to follow along as best she could

Alice went back to the pages to try and figure out what she needed to do. There were so many words she could use and Alice had to go back to find the description of the Jabberwocky in order to figure out which ones were right. The book said that it was just a bunch of words and movements of her hands and thoughts in her mind that she would have to coordinate in order to make the creatures do what she wanted, which seemed a little too simple to her except for the sheer amount of language available that she didn't understand.

Adrianna was still there talking her through it and trying to help her figure out. They talked back and forth, Alice eventually starting to scribble out the words that looked most important in the book and Adrianna using her notes to try and help cobble them all together into phrases that she could actually try to use.

It took them until well into the night, and Alice wasn't

happy about forfeiting a night of looking for the Jabber-wocky, but this was more important. By the end, they cobbled together a few lines that might work out if they understood the book correctly.

It was more than she had before. Tomorrow night, she would try to catch the Jabberwocky.

Chapter 7

Hunting for Monsters

"Do you know where you're going to look tonight?" Adrianna asked as Alice gathered up her notes and threw on a coat. It was curfew and her bed was already filled with pillows in case anyone came to check.

"Mark said Trevor saw something in the woods."

"Is that why they're closed? We weren't allowed to go into them."

Alice nodded. "They think it's a bear, but he also heard the screaming, so I think it was actually the Jabberwocky. That's the last I've heard of it, though, so maybe it moved."

"I hope it's not a bear," Adrianna said. "Wait, so you saw my brother? Did he...?" she reached under her collar and pulled out a small necklace with a metal bit with a Mesopotamian symbol stamped into it on the end.

Alice pulled hers out too, smiling. "Heather got a bunch."

Alice said. She waved before pulling her hood up over her head. "I'll be back soon. Maybe."

She stepped away and was in the forest. Her boots hit the slush and mud, the rain having already washed away most of the snow and creating an awful ground to walk on. She could still see the school from here, as well as the pond where Cat stayed last semester. With the darkness and the backlight of the school, that tree looked almost eerie over the completely black pond, moving and waving in the rain as the drops played among the empty branches.

She took a breath and started into the forest. She pulled out her small flashlight to guide her, looking out for anything that might be a problem. Teachers, bears, anything at all that might make her want to get out of there. Even the Jabberwocky if she didn't think she could do it when they came face to face. Still, she reminded herself as she gripped the pieces of paper in her pocket, she might have a fighting chance.

The lure. She would try that as soon as she was certain that nothing was going to catch her and she found a good place. She wandered the forest until she couldn't see the school anymore and found a section that was wet without being mushy. It had a bit of a canopy to keep the papers from getting wet while Alice tried to read them. She sat on a rock and tried to see what she could make out of the two pages, flashlight in hand.

She was shivering both from the cold and the thought of facing the Jabberwocky. If it didn't work, that would be fine. She was trying magic words to make a creature from another world do what she wanted. There was no way to know if it was going to work at all for her here.

Her father would lock her away if he knew what she was doing right now.

After a deep breath, she looked down and read the words once more. Looking at them now, Alice had no idea how to pronounce any of them properly. It looked like it was in German or some European language she'd never heard before.

Ábedecian bealu gásric ælwiht hércyme

"A… a-beddy-see-an be-a-lou gas-rick al-wit her-sci-me?" she tried. Anxiously, she looked up and around for anything that might have moved in her direction. She was ready to jump at any hint of something moving, anything at all, but there was only the rain. She waited there for a few moments, but still there was nothing.

She let out a breath and got up off the rock. She would try again later, but for now she would move somewhere else. It said in her notes that she would have to make sure it could hear her and it might not be anywhere near here.

As she walked, she got the feeling of something following her. She kept looking, but there were only shadows. Still, she could feel it with every step. The words couldn't have worked. She missed several parts of it, like envisioning what she wanted to happen when she said it. She did it wrong, so there was no way.

She didn't really want it coming close to her at all. Not now. Not in the dark. She needed to do this during the daylight hours.

Something was following her. It watched her and hid as soon as she turned back. It didn't seem malicious, but she couldn't be certain. Just in case, she took out the second piece of paper and tried to figure out how to pronounce it.

Ábedecian héafodwóþ bealu gásric ælwiht sugian

At least half of the words here were the same. If she could think of pure silence and close her hand into a fist at the creature and say the words, then she would be able to keep it quiet and not scream like the creature had been doing so far.

She should head back. She wasn't even trying to get these words right. Though she made a show of trying to do something about it, she was still too scared to face it.

It was her responsibility to put it away, but was it really doing any real harm? Sure, it escaped the book and it used to steal hearts from people, but what had it really done since coming to Lucena Academy? Screamed a few times and scared a couple people. No one was dying. No one went missing. It was just scaring a few people and making people think that maybe there was a ghost.

Maybe she could just leave it. When it did something actually malicious, then she could do something. It was still innocent. Except for the hearts. Really, there was no need to be this worried about a creature that wasn't doing anything wrong.

"Evan, where are we going?"

Alice turned off her flashlight and hid behind a tree. She looked out and saw two figures under an umbrella with heavy boots on. Evan was laughing and leading a girl in a rain coat through the woods by her hand.

"Trust me, I know a place."

"But weren't they looking for bears in here?"

"They're finished. Forest is open again in the morning. But until then, we have it all to ourselves."

"The cold and the mud is real romantic, Ev."

Alice smiled. So that's where the triplets got it from. She looked back, hearing something else skittering away through the forest. She jumped at the sound of it, landing heavy in the mud, but it didn't deter Evan and the girl from whatever they were doing. The skittering got fainter, running away from where Evan and the girl were going. Alice breathed a sigh of relief. If it wasn't even going to go after them, then what did she have to worry about?

Or maybe the skittering was just a squirrel and there was nothing out there at all.

Alice got up, covered in mud and slush and cold. She didn't want to get sick, and she knew if she stayed like this for long she definitely would. In a step, she was back in her dorm room, dripping and tracking mud on the small landing mat.

"Did you find it already?" Adrianna asked, putting down her book and turning down the music. She looked surprised to find Alice back already. "It's not even half an hour. Did you slip?"

"Sort of," Alice said, stripping off the coat and boots to find that underneath, she was still muddy and soaked. "I'll tell you all about it, but I need a shower."

Alice washed away the cold and the dirt on her and let her mind wander. Yes, she was going to let the creature do whatever it wanted for now. Really, what harm was it doing besides scaring people? Nothing. There was no need for her to face it. It would all be fine without her.

She knew she was lying to herself. She let this thing escape to here and it wasn't meant to be here. She didn't know what it was actually doing. If it fed on hearts before — who knew what it was feeding on now? It didn't even eat the hearts it stole before. The Queen kept them like trophies in that room, beating over and over again.

"Alice?" Adrianna called into the bathroom. "Is everything okay?"

"Yeah," Alice said, looking out to the mirror in the bathroom. She could see Wonderland on the other side and knew that Adrianna was probably catching glimpses of it herself. She tried to steer her thoughts away from that and into something a little nicer, but she could only think of the Jabberwocky following behind her.

Why did it run when Evan and that girl went through the woods? She didn't know why they would be there so late after curfew with the weather so terrible, but if the thing following her was the Jabberwocky, it had three excellent sources of food there that it ran away from — including her. Maybe it was just yelling to keep people away.

Alice knew she should send it back to Wonderland. It was where it was from and it knew what to do with itself there. Maybe it didn't eat hearts at all, but something else. That, or they could sic it on the Queen of Hearts and make her stop whatever she was doing.

It shouldn't be left here. It was a creature of madness with those screams, which meant that it should be back in Wonderland where it could be with the other mad people. And Alice would stay here where no one was mad.

When she finally got out of the shower, her fingers were wrinkled. She dressed and tried her best to dry her hair before she walked out of the bathroom to Adrianna, who was anxiously awaiting the story.

"I don't know how to pronounce these things," Alice started, laughing a little as she went to pull the pages, now wet and a little muddy, out of her coat pockets. She laid them out on the desk to dry and Adrianna laughed along with her.

"How did you not notice that while you were writing?"

Alice shrugged. "You could say them, so I thought I could too. It didn't work, but I think it found me anyway. It just kind of followed me and didn't do anything. It was weird."

"Nothing?" Adrianna asked. "I guess it doesn't remember that you let it out before. But that's good, right? If it doesn't scream, then it doesn't have a chance to scare you! And if you aren't scared, then you can still do stuff. Did you try the second one?"

Alice shook her head. "No, I let it stay there. I couldn't even pronounce the first one and I really didn't want to make it mad enough to get close and not be able to pronounce the second one. Imagine if it actually remembered me and I made it mad, especially since I still don't know what I'm going to do with it when I catch it."

"Maybe find something about putting it back in the book?"

"I think I'm just going to send it back to Wonderland," Alice said. "That's where the book is from, anyway. I think next time I'll try it during the day. Besides, I wanted to get out of there before anyone caught me. I just missed Evan and this girl he was with going through the forest. I don't know why they were out there in the rain, though."

"Evan?" Adrianna asked. "Do I know him?"

CHAPTER 8

Stakes Raised

ADRIANNA HAD SIX brothers: Ryan, Joseph, Travis, Mike, Mark and, Matt. According to anyone Alice tried to ask about it, Evan had never existed. There was no Treasurer on the Student Council and Alice didn't know where else to go to find out if he ever existed. The computers? She didn't know the first thing about tracking someone down in a computer.

The closest she got to anyone acknowledging that Evan had ever existed was Kevin saying he sort of remembered that there was a Treasurer on the Student Council once and that they had even seen him, but he couldn't come up with any more detail than that. He ended up brushing it off as something he imagined.

Her only lead was stories of the girl in the raincoat. Her name was Amy and she had heard the scream when she was walking back to the dormitories. Alice wanted to ask her why she was out in the forest and if she'd seen anything or knew anyone named Evan, but with her in the high school it was impossible to do so without seeming strange.

Alice regretted letting the Jabberwocky go that night. She worried what it meant for every other time someone had heard it. Was someone going missing every time, falling prey to the Jabberwocky?

She wracked her brain to try and figure out who might have gone missing that night in the library. Was there a librarian missing? Maybe a page who was there late sorting through the books. And from the first day — who was missing from that time? Had Trevor been wandering through the woods with someone else a week ago that was now gone forever?

Panic settled in. Now she knew someone was missing — taken by the Jabberwocky. She didn't want to believe they were dead. It was too awful to think that they might be dead and no one remembered that they ever lived in the first place.

And if no one remembered, should she even tell them that they were missing? Adrianna would worry and probably be sad if she knew she had a brother that she couldn't remember. Worse, she would be mad because it was Alice's fault he was gone.

She had to find the Jabberwocky now. It was making people disappear, and not just physically. It took their memories with them and, even if Alice couldn't bring them back, she needed to make sure that it did not take anyone else. There was at least a week between from each sighting of the ghost, which meant that she had some time to work with. All she needed to do was get to it before next week.

"It's Old English," Adrianna said when she peered over Alice's shoulder the next morning, taking one of the sheets of paper and looking it over. "We're learning a couple songs in Old English for choir."

"Can you teach me to say them?" Alice asked. She would hold off on telling Adrianna for now about her missing brother, though she felt guilty asking her to help without mentioning it.

"Yeah. This one is *ábedecian beal...*"

That glossy look returned over her eyes as she started saying the second word and she succumbed to it, stumbling back and landing hard on the ground. Alice rushed to her side as she sat there, dazed for a minute until she realized what was going on again. Adrianna laughed.

"I guess that book really doesn't like me," she said. "Maybe just take it one word at a time?"

"You don't have to do this," Alice said quickly, helping Adrianna back up to her feet. She was shaky, but fine a moment later.

Adrianna took one of the sheets of paper and went to sit on her bed. "It's probably because I'm not supposed to be learning spells like you are, but I think I can do one word at a time. Okay, so the first one is pronounced *ábedecian*."

Adrianna spent a good half hour with Alice every morning until the weekend trying to go through and learn how to pronounce every word on the pages. Alice wasn't used to any of the sounds or the places in her mouth where they came from, but she finally managed to at least passably stumble through all of the accents and pronunciations until they kind of made sense.

Once she was comfortable with the words, Alice tried changing one of the spells around a little and Adrianna helped her figure out the new words in it. It wouldn't summon the Jabberwocky, but something a little bit closer and only marginally less dangerous.

"*Ábedecian gliwere snytrian eormencynn hércyme.*" She pictured them coming to the door as she spoke.

She felt a bit of a tingle run up the back of her neck when three identical people appeared in the doorway. All three of Adrianna's brothers had come from different directions to their door and leaned in. They all looked a little confused about having shown up, but more curious and trying to puzzle it out rather than asking one another what was going on.

"Hey," Matt said first, looking to Adrianna and Alice. "Um... so."

"We were just going to go see Joe," Mike said quickly. "Did you want to come with?"

Adrianna started laughing first, followed by Alice. The matching looks of confusion were priceless and Alice was grateful that it worked.

"Let me get my coat," Adrianna said. "Alice, you want to come too?"

"Sure," Alice said, her heart sinking a little. She worried that one of them might remember Evan and she didn't want to have to tell them that he was gone. Not dead, she decided. There had to be a way to get him back, but she didn't know how she was going to do that yet. "Why are you going to see Joe?"

"He heard the ghost last night," Mark said. "We plan on teasing him about it as much as family should."

Alice hesitated to pull her coat on the rest of the way. It was still filthy from falling, but at least it was dry now. She thought she had more time, but another already? They were too close to each other and she wasn't ready. She needed to get back out and look for the Jabberwocky. Evan said that the forest was opening, which meant they must have caught something in the woods. Or maybe the Jabberwocky had caught them.

"What about Travis?" Alice asked, hoping that they would still remember him. She hoped that Joe hadn't been with his twin when he heard it. She couldn't handle the guilt of losing two of Adrianna's brothers.

"I don't think he heard anything yet," Mike said. Alice breathed a sigh of relief. At least it wasn't Travis.

"You guys don't still believe it's a ghost, right?" Alice asked as they made their way out across the campus to the high school dorms. "So what do you think Joe saw?"

They shrugged. "He's reasonable, though. He'll probably be able to tell us when we get there. Apparently there was a whole group of them heading back to the dorms when they heard it and Joe was with them all. It's everyone else calling it a ghost, but Joe's got to have a better explanation for it."

"I hope so," Matt said. "Otherwise people aren't going to buy our stuff if our own brother heard the thing. Though we could just say we didn't give him one."

"It would help us save face. And I do like having a nice steady income."

The dorms for the high school were larger than the middle school ones and much louder. The triplets led them through a back door, which connected with the rest of the dorms and led them through a less densely populated part of the halls to their brother's room. Among the rest of the building, they could hear people, music blaring and general noise from the boy's side, but down here was quiet enough.

Alice found herself wondering what Evan's room would

look like now that he didn't exist anymore. Would it still be there, now occupied by someone else, or would it be empty except for all of his stuff? If someone saw his stuff, would they remember that he existed again?

They knocked on the door, Joe opening it a moment later. "What are you guys doing here?" he asked, eyes narrowing as he looked over the triplet's faces. "What did you do?"

"If we did something, we wouldn't have brought Addie along,"

Joe looked more confused when they moved out of the way to show that Addie and Alice were both there. Alice got the distinct impression that this idea to go visit their brother hadn't actually been an idea at all, just an excuse that they were passing off as a plan to save face.

Joe moved out of the way and let them file into the dorm room that he shared with Travis. It was immediately apparent who lived on which side of the room. Sports stuff was thrown on one side and different posters covered the walls. Travis' side was considerably more colourful while Joe's was covered in much darker band posters. Alice recognized a few on both sides from Lori's room.

"So... what's up?" Joe asked, closing his laptop and turning off the music he was listening to. It was something with a lot of drums, guitar and angry sounding people that no one seemed to be the least bit surprised by. He also grabbed his phone and started pressing buttons on it before putting it back on his desk.

"Can't we visit our big brother?"

"You can," he said. "But you usually don't unless you've done something. And if you're bringing Addie and Alice along, it has to have been something big. So you start talking and try not to piss me off too much."

"Always so suspicious, Joe."

"We heard that you saw the ghost. We just wanted to make sure you're okay. Like family."

Joe rolled his eyes and dropped into his large, black computer chair that spun and looked more comfortable than the chairs Alice and Adrianna had at their desks in their room. "That?" he asked. "I'd rather forget it, really. It happened, it's over, the myth of the ghost goes on. I just can't believe no one's fessed up about pulling the prank. Actually, I can't believe it's not you guys."

"We can't believe it's not us either," Matt said, smiling. "But do you think it's the same people every time? To pull off something like this, you have to be fast and more than a few people. And it's happening everywhere."

"I don't know what it is, guys," Joe said, shaking his head. "I just want to know how they're doing it. I do not know how a scream freaked me out as much as that one did. A couple of you guys heard it back at the start of all this, right? Mark?"

Mark nodded, still looking a little shaken by the memory. "It's probably just the frequency. If you hit it just right, you can do some weird stuff. Which means they have to get the really good quality speakers, which are crazy hard to deal with. You can't move those fast."

"I bet it was a couple seniors the first time," Matt said. "They checked the dorms and the attic to try and figure out who did it, but they didn't find anything and everyone was back in their dorms when they checked. No one missing at all. All heads accounted for."

Alice looked away at that one. All heads they remembered, maybe. She didn't notice any empty seats from her classes, so maybe no one. Not from her year. She couldn't be sure that no one else was gone just because no one she knew was missing. She sat in the corner next to Adrianna and resisted the urge to curl up into a small ball and hide. She didn't want to deal with this right now.

The door opened and Travis came in, looking a little worried, but more irritated. "What's the— oh."

"Sorry, false alarm," Joe said. "They aren't in trouble."

"For once," Travis said, kicking off his shoes and throwing them to his side of the room. He was about to close the door behind them, but hesitated looking around the room. "Should I...?"

"We're family, it's fine," Joe said.

"Except her," Travis said, pointing out Alice in the corner.

Joe turned to her. "Alice, can you move a little bit to your right? And just stay there until you go?"

Alice, puzzled, shuffled over a little to the right.

Joe nodded to Travis, who shook his head and closed the door with a smile. "Not ready to deal with someone's bullshit today?" Travis asked, taking a seat on his bed and grinning wide.

"And guess what they're here about," Joe said, sighing.

Travis laughed and shook his head. "Since it happened, Joe's become a bit of a celebrity."

"In a week, they will stop."

"He hopes."

"In a week it had better be over," Joe said. "God, everyone else already said everything about what happened, so you'd think they'd forget about me, but of course not. I was the dumbass that decided that, hey, maybe I'll suggest that this whole thing is faked somehow and there's a reasonable explanation."

"And now you have the amateur ghost hunters asking for a sound bite."

"I just wish this would be over already!"

"Sorry it wasn't us," Mike said, trying not to laugh too hard at his brother's pain. "But we have a strict no family policy."

"Unless it's personal," Travis pointed out.

"But who has access to fancy equipment that's actually portable enough to be pulling this everywhere?"

"You guys figured out how they did it?"

"Almost," Matt said. "We figure it's a speaker with a couple key frequencies hit on the scream to give it the extra bad feeling down your spine and the weird psychotropic stuff, but you need a really high quality speaker to have that work."

"Did you hear about Amy, though? Apparently she heard it in the middle of the field on the way back to the dorms. Not a lot of places to plug in a high quality speaker around there. Unless you can think of one that's portable that can do all of that. And since when does the screaming cause hallucinations?"

Their eyes went to the people who'd actually heard it. Joe and Mark went quiet, as did Adrianna and Alice. The other three waited for some answer on the whole matter, but none of them were feeling that talkative. Alice couldn't remember talking to anyone about it after either time, come to think of it. There was a councillor available, but she was not on good terms with anyone that wanted to know what was happening in her brain.

"It was scary," Adrianna offered, her voice small. The first time, that's all it was. Scary. Alice's mind went to the second time, where scary was only the start of it.

"It was a bit worse than that," Joe told them. "It was

almost like all the worst things I could think of were happening at once. Anything that might have caused the screaming that I thought could be happening was actually happening. I just kept cycling through every horrible way someone could get murdered and it was terrifying. I mean, Carrie was out cold after it stopped. We were all looking around to make sure everyone was okay." Joe shook his head. "If there's a sound frequency that can do that to you, I'm surprised it isn't being used by the military because I know for damn sure I couldn't do a thing."

Alice couldn't help but curl up, bringing her knees to her chest as Joe talked. She could still remember the beating hearts. They were there again, just in memory, all around her. She was tried to push the memory away, though the hearts would not stop.

Adrianna nudged her. Alice looked up and followed her eyes to something reflective on the ground. In it, she could see the violet eyes of the cat staring back at her.

"Maybe it was someone with connections?" Mike suggested. "I mean, it has to be something like that, right? What else could it even be? And if it were us, that's probably how we'd do it."

"I doubt it's just sound, though," Joe said. "There might be some chemical mixed in with the whole thing. Maybe a bit of a mist goes into the air and the speakers play and somewhere, someone is gauging the reactions, adjusting the dosages and frequencies just a little bit. They have a project that needs testing and what better place to test than an isolated place like Lucena Academy? No one will think to check here. Bunch of rich kids, so they'll blame it on drugs and partying. Pay off the right people and no one will even think twice about it. And meanwhile, they have a whole campus full of students to test their newest weapon on."

"Okay, now I know you're screwing with us," Mike said.

Joe relaxed and sat back in his chair with a shrug and a bit of a laugh. "But you gotta admit, that would be a great start to a horror movie. Right before everyone turns into zombies."

"Looks like you're going to give Alice nightmares," Travis said, looking over to find Alice staring off into the distance all curled up. "You okay?"

Alice caught sight of what was behind the purple eyes, which left as soon as they realized where they were. She stared at that room of still beating hearts, pulsing over and over again. She could almost hear throbbing in her head. The beating never left, always in the back of her mind and getting louder.

Adrianna nudged Alice to no effect. She glanced over at the reflection and saw what Alice saw, though did a good job of looking immediately away instead of really registering what it was. Or maybe she just saw red and didn't think anything of it at all.

"Hey," Travis said, tapping Alice on the head. "You still in there?"

Alice jumped when he touched her, thinking it was a drop of something dripping from the room coming through. She looked up and saw Travis and everyone else looking genuinely concerned. Alice tried to laugh a little, though it came out small and nervous.

"Sorry," she said. "I was just... remembering something." She glanced back, but the hearts weren't gone yet. There were so many more than before.

"Yeah, I don't think I'm going to forget that screaming any time soon," Joe said, smiling sympathetically. "Just a couple seconds and I don't think I slept at all last night."

"It's worse the second time," Alice said, still distracted by the hearts.

"What?"

"Alice heard it again," Adrianna said, nudging Alice hard in the side to get her to pay attention again. "It was a while ago, though. She didn't want to worry anyone."

"Good idea," Joe said, shaking his head. "I wish I thought of that. It could have saved me a lot of trouble."

"Was it before or after we gave you that charm?" Mark asked, looking over at her sidelong.

"You mean the charm that you made Heather pay for?" Alice countered. She tore her eyes away from the room. "Before."

"Wait, wait," Travis said. "Hold up."

"What are you selling on campus without permission?" Joe asked.

"They're just some charms," Mike said. "You know, to keep the ghost away. No big deal. We made a bunch of them and it's not like we're charging that much for them."

"You can't be charging *at all*," Travis said. "You guys know that. You can't keep pulling this shit on campus. You are going to get caught and we won't be able to bail you out. I don't know how you guys haven't gotten suspended already with the crap you keep trying."

"What if you joined Student Council?" Mark suggested. "Then you could bail us out whenever you wanted."

"I heard there was an opening for a treasurer," Alice suggested. She watched their faces when she said it. The triplets seemed to accept this at face value, while Travis wasn't happy that she was helping them with their suggestion that they help get their brothers out of trouble.

Joe, on the other hand, thought about it for a minute. "Isn't there...?" he asked, though let it drop there. "Huh, I guess there isn't. I could have sworn there was a guy doing it earlier this year."

None of them remembered. None of them.

She let the boys continue to try and convince Joe and Travis to try to go for the empty position, despite the fact that the council was not looking to fill it and were running fine without it. The older brothers tried to convince the younger ones to just stop doing things that were going to get them in trouble, to an equal lack of success.

It continued until there was a knock on the door. Alice shuffled further to the right, ducking her head behind Travis' bed and Joe went to answer the door. "Yes?" he asked, sounding completely unhappy and annoyed when he opened it.

"Hey Joe," the person on the other side of the door said. She sounded both peppy and nervous, her words stumbling out one after another as she spoke. "We were just wondering, since you were there last night and all, if you could please come out with us and tell us about—"

"Can't you see I'm busy?" he asked. Joe let the door drift open wider so she could clearly see that there were people in his room with him. She heard a few of his brothers mutter greetings, probably waving when they did so.

"Is she from the middle school?" she asked, sounding very accusing.

"You mean my sister?"

"Sister?"

"Yep. Goodbye."

The door closed and Alice stayed with her head down for a few moments until Joe sat back down. "I might just keep you guys here all day," Joe said.

"Or you could stop answering the door," Travis suggested.

"Are you going to start remembering your key?"

"I'll text."

"Are you going to keep remembering your phone? It was a fluke you answered it."

"You have no faith."

"With good reason."

"You can't keep us here, anyway," Matt said. "We have stuff to do."

"That's a good point," Travis said. "If we keep them here, then they can't do anything to get in trouble."

"That's it, we're busting out of here. Come on, girls," Mark said, getting up. Everyone else that didn't belong in that dorm did the same, getting to their feet with no protest from Joe or Travis.

"Hey," Travis said as Alice straightened herself up. "Have you heard anything about Lori?"

Alice shook her head, though the memory of her made things a little sadder. She needed to figure out where Lori had gone and why her parents wouldn't speak of her, but one thing at a time. She needed to figure out how to get their brother back and make them all remember him first.

"Nothing?" he pressed.

"She didn't come home for Christmas," Alice said. "No calls, nothing."

"Did your parents say anything?"

"I'm not supposed to ask about her anymore," she said, inching her way towards the door with everyone else. "I don't know what's going on or what happened to her. I'm sorry."

The look Travis gave her was closer to pity than anything else, but Alice didn't question it. She left with everyone out the back door, out of the high school dorms and out into the bright day.

CHAPTER 9

Facing the Jabberwocky

ALICE AND ADRIANNA went off to wander the campus instead of tagging along with her brothers. Alice wasn't quite right after looking back into the room of hearts and she needed the sunshine to remind her that she wasn't going back.

She managed to force herself to think of something else, her mind now going to how none of them remembered their brother. Joe got about as close as Kevin did to remembering Evan's existence, but no one else. Not even that little glimmer that it might have been their brother; just that there was someone who used to do that on the council and nothing more.

Maybe she should have pressed a little more. Maybe if she tried harder, Joe might have been able to remember what was missing and actually been able to put a name to it. Or he wouldn't be able to and Alice would be right back to where she was now.

Tell them or don't tell them that their brother was probably victim to a creature they didn't even know existed? Or maybe she should go and try to find the Jabberwocky right now, figure out how to get him back and not worry about any of this.

It was probably still in the forest. She could go right now and use those spells to make it come out to her. She knew the words and she knew that they worked. After all, she had gotten Adrianna's brothers to show up, so finding it in the forest now would be easy. Once she had it, it would just be a matter of silencing it and then sending it away into Wonderland. It couldn't be that hard to find a mirror and she was sure the Queen would enjoy seeing her old pet again.

She wondered if the Jabberwocky would return to being the Queen's pet.

"Alice?" Adrianna asked, grabbing Alice by the arm.

Alice looked up and saw that they were across the field and almost at the forest. "Sorry," she said. "I was just thinking."

"You've been kind of weird all day," she said. "Since you got back from the Jabberwocky, too. Have you been reading the book without me?"

"No," Alice said quickly. "It's just... something else happened." Alice let out a sigh. She should just tell Adrianna. She owed her that much.

"What?" Adrianna asked.

Alice didn't look at her, not sure she was ready to take the looks she was going to be getting. She'd think Alice was crazy. She'd deny any of it. It would all be in Alice's head.

When she did, Alice would pretend it was a joke. She was sure she could convince Adrianna that she wasn't serious. At the very least she knew that, if she asked, Adrianna wouldn't tell anyone about it and keep the fact that Alice believed in people no one remembered a secret.

"Evan," Alice said. "You have a brother named Evan. He is the Treasurer on the Student Council and he kept your brothers in school when they got to be too much trouble. When I was out that night, I saw him and that Amy girl. They were in the forest and I saw the Jabberwocky, but I thought it was running away from them. And then Amy heard that scream and came back, but no one could remember who Evan was. No one was ever on the Student Council as Treasurer. And you didn't have an older brother. No one can remember him. Well, Joe almost did. He knew there was someone, but he couldn't quite put it together."

The words kept falling out of Alice's mouth and she took a small breath. She couldn't let herself get emotional now. "I didn't know how to tell you. I had no idea the Jabberwocky could do that, because stuff like that's not supposed to happen here. I guess it could happen in Wonderland, but not here. I just didn't know how to tell you."

Alice still didn't look up. She was already coming up with the best way to laugh it off when she looked back up at her. Just a moment longer and she could smile and...

"I have another brother?"

Alice looked up and saw that Adrianna was more bewildered than anything. She wasn't even looking at Alice, instead straining to remember him, but the answer eluded her like the date on a History test.

At first, Alice thought she was humouring her, but she knew Adrianna wouldn't do that. She was not her brothers.

"I met him the first day I came to Lucena Academy," Alice said, hoping it would help. She wanted Adrianna to remember, if only so she could have her back as someone to confide in. "He helped me get up to my room and he introduced me to you."

Adrianna kept trying for a long moment before she shook her head. "I don't remember," she said, but she looked sad about it. "I don't really remember what happened very well. I remember talking to you, and I remember being alone for a bit before you came, but I can't really remember when you came in. I'm trying to think, but there's a lot of empty spots. It's hard to think about them."

"It's okay," Alice said, seeing that Adrianna was starting to panic. Alice put her hand on Adrianna's shoulders and tried to turn Adrianna to look at her. She hoped this meant that she didn't think Alice was crazy. She hoped this was enough. "It's because the Jabberwocky got him. But I think I can get it to let them go."

"Them?" Adrianna asked. "Are there more brothers that I have that I can't remember?"

"No," Alice said. "But every time the Jabberwocky attacks someone, I think the screaming means that he's taking someone else. Which means he's probably got a lot of people by now and I have to stop him before he takes more."

"He must have been hungry," Adrianna agreed. She headed back towards the forest. "You said he's in the forest last time, right?"

"Wait, what are you doing?" Alice asked, falling in step next to her.

"Going with you to find the Jabberwocky," she said. "If he took my brother, I'm going to help."

"But it's dangerous," Alice said. "You could get hurt!"

"You'll help me escape if it gets scary," Adrianna said confidently. "So how should we catch it?"

Alice smiled. No questions, no hesitations, Adrianna believed her. It was the first time it had ever happened and Alice couldn't remember feeling so relieved in her life. Even

Lori, who accepted that something might have once happened to Alice, never quite seemed to believe everything. That anyone would believe her so easily, Alice didn't think a moment like this would ever come.

On the other hand, she didn't want Adrianna to disappear too. If anything happened, she could grab Adrianna and pull her away back to the dorms and then come back to deal with it, but she would have to be quick enough to make sure it didn't scream first. The spells came into her mind and she started reciting them in her head over and over, trying to make sure she was ready before they found it.

"I'll try to lure it out," Alice said, her voice sounding a lot more confident than she felt about it. "And when we see it, I'll make it quiet so it can't scream. Then I guess we try to make it bring us to where it's keeping everyone?"

And before that, I get you back to the dorms, Alice added to herself.

"You'll figure something out," Adrianna told her. Alice worried about how certain she sounded.

Adrianna was the one that led the way into the woods. It was still muddy, but the puddles were easy to avoid in the daylight and the ground was a lot more solid than when Alice was last here. They looked around before venturing past the first couple rows of trees to make sure they weren't being watched going in. While it was not technically off limits, there were usually people who would tell them that they shouldn't be wandering around the forest bordering the school on their own. It was much larger than most people realized and very easy to get lost if they went off the path.

Alice stopped Adrianna when she looked back and couldn't see the school through the trees any more. She didn't want to get too far into the forest if they could help it. If something horrible happened — if the Jabberwocky took Alice and left Adrianna alone in the woods with no memory of how she got there — then at least Adrianna could get back on her own.

She could also feel the eyes. Something watched them from deep in the woods and Alice was already apprehensive about what she was about to do. She needed more time to prepare, but Adrianna looked so determined. And she trusted Alice. She couldn't let her down now.

"Here should be good," Alice said, stopping them in enough of a clearing that they could both walk around in it, but not so big that they would have to run far to duck behind one of the trees. With Adrianna here, Alice found herself a lot more nervous and worried that this was all a bad idea. She would need to make sure that Adrianna didn't do anything to draw its attention. She hoped Adrianna would run.

Alice hoped that she wouldn't run herself.

Alice looked around again, knowing it was hesitation that kept her from just going for it. Adrianna was still standing there, staring expectantly out into the woods like she was waiting for something to come out. She wasn't looking in the right direction, though. Alice knew where it was and knew where it would come out when she called. She really didn't want to call.

Adrianna looked back at her. She knew the look on her face. She was waiting for Alice to do something, to summon the monster and defeat it and get her forgotten brother back. Alice was more worried that she didn't know what she was getting into, but moved closer to her anyway.

If the monster came, she'd wait until they could actually see it and then get Adrianna out of there. If she saw the Jabberwocky, that would be enough to convince her that Alice was telling her the truth.

"Okay, are you ready?" Alice asked. Her heart pounded in her chest as she went over exactly what she'd do if it came. Adrianna nodded, smiling her encouraging smile and looking at Alice like she was going to fix everything for her.

Here went everything.

"*Ábedecian bealu gásric ælwiht hércyme,*" Alice said, her voice carrying farther than she thought it would. She thought of the Jabberwocky following her that night. Instead of letting the dangerous creature stay over there and mind its own business, Alice was calling it over whether it wanted to visit or not.

There was a crack in the middle of the forest, followed by

another one. While Alice was in the midst of trying to keep herself from bolting, Adrianna watched as the dark shape in the distant woods started bounding closer.

Alice managed to clear her mind, though only because they were probably doomed if she didn't. The next spell was on the tip of her tongue and her mind. She waited until the creature got close enough to hear her properly.

The dark shape drew closer and closer. It hit trees and she could hear it cracking branches and crushing bushes, the rustling surely enough to attract some attention from the campus, but she didn't hear anything coming their way. Whatever it was, it was dark brown like the deepest parts of the woods and big enough to fill a classroom.

When it was close enough that Alice thought she could yell at it, panic surged through her as she realized that the Jabberwocky was about to crash through the trees. Alice held out a hand and tried to keep her mind quiet, which wasn't hard because the blind panic taking over her wouldn't let anything enter her mind.

She stuck her hand out towards the Jabberwocky. "*Ábedecian héafodwóþ bealu gásric ælwiht sugian!*" she yelled. She closed her hand and threw her fist to the side just in time. The neck of it stretched forward and Alice got a look at it for the first time as it opened its toothy maw to let out a silent cry. It looked like a dragon with its mouth on sideways and set in its face instead of sticking out in a snout. It was huge, at least as large as the clearing she chose and definitely large enough that Alice knew that they were no match. It had large claws and a spindly body that looked like it was strong enough to tear them in two.

And it was picking up speed.

Adrianna didn't move, but Alice didn't think it would stop. It only got faster and it was almost upon them. The claws ripped at the sides of the trees as it pushed through them. Alice looked at Adrianna and the Jabberwocky, almost positive that it was staring at her as it bounded forward.

"This was a bad idea," Alice said, grabbing Adrianna and pulling her along a few steps back into their dorm room. "We need to come up with a better plan than— Adrianna?"

Alice looked back to find that Adrianna hadn't come back with her. Her hand was empty, but she didn't feel Adrianna tug away. She just wasn't there anymore, and Alice was panicking. Did she leave her behind? Did the creature already get her? If she went back, was she going to regret what she saw?

CHAPTER 10

Game Over

SHE TOOK A few steps and went back to the clearing, looking in from the edge of it to the Jabberwocky taking up the entire space. It paced back and forth, the wings behind it looking just as deadly as the claws. They were folded up now, though Alice could see spikes at the bottom of them where they were starting to unfurl to make it look even bigger.

At the centre of its attention was Adrianna, standing there and watching in the middle of the clearing. She hadn't moved since Alice left and her eyes were on the Jabberwocky, studying it as it studied her. She wasn't backing down and Alice thought that she might be able to slip in and try to pull her out again.

She couldn't bring herself to move, terrified that drawing its attention would mean that it would focus on her instead. She could run, but it kept getting closer to Adrianna, ready to strike. It took another step and Alice leaned forward. She couldn't let Adrianna get taken by it — not when she was the only one who believed her. Alice started forward when Adrianna spoke.

"Sit!" Adrianna told it sternly.

The Jabberwocky slammed its rear onto the ground and sat up straight, wings fully folded and tail curled obediently around it. It bent down to Adrianna, who patted it on the spiny head. Its tail twitched and it looked content, lying down fully in front of Adrianna and letting her continue.

Alice blinked at the scene. Did that just happen? That couldn't have happened.

"Alice!" Adrianna said. She didn't seem mad that Alice had accidentally abandoned her when this dragon attacked them, instead waving her over. "I don't think he's dangerous!"

Alice looked between the Jabberwocky and Adrianna, finally settling on the Jabberwocky. It stayed down, looking content now that Adrianna was paying attention to it. This was the creature that had been attacking students all over campus, making people forget that they ever existed and possibly even ate them. It was the size of a classroom, with sharp, gnashing teeth and claws that left deep marks in the trees that Alice could see from here. This was the ghost that left so many people missing, possibly eaten and several more scarred in a way that some people would likely never get over.

Somehow, Alice was pretty sure this thing was still dangerous.

Adrianna seemed sure that it was fine, so Alice moved slowly, trying not to make any sudden movements as she got closer. The Jabberwocky shifted as Alice got close, smelling the air with the slits it had for a nose up between its eyes and down along the top of its mouth. Alice wasn't sure if it could see her, but she was very sure that it smelled her.

The Jabberwocky got up as soon as it thought she was too close and spun around, back on all four legs and moved like it was guarding Adrianna. It started to unfurl its wings and lowered its head down towards Alice, all of its teeth bared and hissing, though no noise came out of it.

Alice jumped back and was about to run to the dorms. Her heart jumped up into her throat, so sure that it was going to bite her head off and devour her and every memory of her that ever existed. She'd never be a disappointment to her father again and Adrianna would never remember her, instead just getting a new pet dragon instead of a friend who abandoned her when she was in danger.

"Hey!" Adrianna snapped at the Jabberwocky. "No. Down. Sit."

The Jabberwocky hesitated, moving back and forth with its long claws scratching at the ground before it finally settled down on the dirt again. It did not lie down this time, instead crouching and staring at Alice.

Alice couldn't take her eyes off of it. It was just as awful as she thought it would be. It even looked like the sort of thing that would let out terrible screams to cause her worst nightmares to happen. "How did you do that?" Alice asked, walking wide around the Jabberwocky and feeling uneasy about it following her with its eyes.

"I just told him to sit," Adrianna said as if it were the most obvious thing in the world. She walked around it to meet Alice and kept a hand on it to help steady herself as she walked over its tail. The Jabberwocky wasn't bothered at all, its eyes still on Alice. She was almost certain that if it weren't silent right now, it would be growling at her.

"I don't think it likes me," Alice said.

"Nothing from Wonderland really likes you, you said," Adrianna said. "So now that we found it, what do we do with it? How do we get everyone back?"

Alice didn't have an answer for that. They had a dragon that would listen to Adrianna that had spent half a semester kidnapping people and making them disappear. "Maybe find out where it lives?" Alice suggested. She turned to look at the creature who would be attacking her if Adrianna wasn't there. "Maybe *you* should ask it where it lives."

"Can you take us back to your home?" Adrianna asked, sounding like she was taking to a dog. "Can you take us to your home? Where's your home?"

The Jabberwocky tilted its head for a moment, looking Adrianna over before bending down and offering her a spot on its neck. Adrianna looked to Alice, who shuffled back when he made any movement close to her.

Adrianna took a step forward, putting an easy hand on its neck. She looked back to Alice, who kept her distance and was trapped in a staring match with the Jabberwocky. It didn't attack her, but she was positive that it didn't like her. It might be purely because of Adrianna that it stayed with her at all. Alice didn't trust it, but so far Adrianna seemed to have the beast completely under control.

Once Adrianna climbed on its neck it took off, leaving Alice alone in the clearing as it bounded through the forest. Adrianna let out a yell, trying to tell it to stop and wait for Alice, but it had her now and it was determined to get rid of Alice by running as fast as it could.

Alice ran after it, focusing ahead of her to places it went. With every step, she had to adjust to where he was now and she was finding herself getting tired of walking and trying to concentrate on where it was going. Inanimate objects she could find easily, even if she had no idea where they were, but moving living things were another matter altogether and she was not going to lose it.

It was tricky because it didn't want to be followed. It extended those wings just a little, not enough that it could fly, not that it could in such tight quarters, but enough that it was knocking into the trees and cutting down the branches as it ran away.

Alice had to keep dodging falling branches and foliage, missteps into boulders, pitfalls, and the sharp turns the Jabberwocky kept taking in an effort to lose her, but she narrowly managed to keep up until it finally came to a cave in the middle of the woods. It stopped abruptly at the entrance of it and looped around in a circle before settling down and letting Adrianna off its neck.

Alice caught up a few moments later, having to take smaller and smaller jumps now because of all the running and tripping and falling. Her hair was knotted with leaves and twigs from the falls and from things falling into her. She was pretty sure she had a few new cuts and scrapes from the tumbles she took, glad that she was in weekend clothing so that she wouldn't have to explain to the school why she had one uniform that was completely ruined.

She was wheezing and out of breath, bending over double

and trying to inhale as much air as she could manage before standing up. Her lungs were on fire from the run and she was light-headed from having to move so fast through the forest. It would be a while before she fully caught her breath, but the Jabberwocky still glared at her like she was a knight sent to kill it. She kept her distance.

"I think you lost something," Adrianna said, trying to keep a smile down as she pointed at Alice's feet. Alice looked down, finding one of her socks soaked through and a shoe missing.

Alice was not amused, reaching backwards and pulling her shoe out of wherever she had dropped it. "Thanks," she said, though she was too tired to sound grateful. She took her sock off and wrung it out, though it wasn't enough to make her put it back on. With a shrug, she dropped her sock altogether, not wanting to put it in a pocket and carry it with her, and put her shoe back on her bare foot. Next adventure, she was bringing boots. She would make Adrianna stop at their dorm and she would get boots. "I really don't think it likes me."

It let out what might have been a huff, as if agreeing with Alice. She shook her head and looked at Adrianna. "You think you could convince it to let us see what's in there?" she asked.

"I think he'll let us just walk in," Adrianna said, leading the way in. Alice stuck to Adrianna, using her as a shield from the Jabberwocky, who followed her with its eyes and long neck and unnatural maw as they went in. Alice never stopped looking at it, ready to run as soon as it tried to do something.

They walked into the cave and Alice was in awe. Her eyes left the Jabberwocky despite it following them in as she looked around at the walls, all of them having turned to glass. They were smooth, reflecting the small pile that probably served as the Jabberwocky's nest.

The nest was made mostly of rocks that had gotten a similar glass treatment, like a sparkling bed of gems to lie on amongst the other things on the ground. Alice was grateful that there were no bones or signs that there was ever a person in here, instead finding things that people might have left in the forest on their own. There were clothes and water bottles and other innocuous items that didn't look like they had any significance at all. The Jabberwocky darted past them to lie on his glass nest. Alice could still see what they were as he curled around them, the reflection in the ceiling giving her a good view.

Underneath his hind leg was an umbrella that she recognized from Evan that night. The print looked the same in the dim light that she could tell from the mouth of the cave. She looked back to Adrianna, not really sure how to tell her and her mind racing to come up with another explanation.

They were in a cave that didn't have any sign that a human had ever been in here besides the trinkets. There were a few bones in the cave kept in the corner, though they all looked like they belonged to animals that were far smaller than any human. Alice still had trouble sorting through any of this to come up with a logical explanation that didn't end with a dead brother.

"Are you sure he's that dangerous?" Adrianna asked, looking around for some sign of people here. "Like, that he really did anything? He seems harmless."

"He's got your brother's umbrella," Alice said, pointing it out in the reflection. "I think he's plenty dangerous. And I don't see any people here."

Adrianna's expression fell as she looked around, finding that there really was nowhere to hide a person.

Alice was at a loss. She had no idea where it was even keeping the people everyone forgot, much less how to get them back. On the other hand, she couldn't let it just keep going. She didn't like it, but she needed to get rid of it and she could figure out what to do about the missing people when it was no longer staring her down.

But there was also Adrianna. She looked lost, hearing that the brother that she couldn't remember was now probably gone forever. She looked like she was trying to remember and rationalize it, to find a way that it would all be okay, but she just couldn't put it together.

Alice had no idea what she was going to do to help Adrianna, but she had some clue about what to do to get rid of the Jabberwocky. It should be easy to get it back to Wonderland, where it would just be taking hearts instead of taking people and the memories of them.

"Are you okay?" Alice asked Adrianna.

Her face was a mask of confusion. "I don't know. Are you sure the Jabberwocky really did it? He doesn't seem like he'd do anything."

"What else could?" Alice asked. "The Jabberwocky came out of that book."

"But you said the book only took hearts," she said, starting to sound desperate. "If it took his heart like it did in Wonderland, then maybe Evan is out there somewhere, just wandering around without his heart and the Jabberwocky has the heart hidden somewhere."

Alice smiled a genuine smile, wide and giddy as she looked up into the walls of the cave. "You're a genius!" Alice said, pressing the flashlight into her hands. "His heart is probably in here somewhere. I can get the Jabberwocky back to Wonderland first, and then we'll find Evan's heart and try to find Evan. He can't be that far from here. Well, he might be, but we can find him."

Adrianna took this as enough, though the Jabberwocky seemed to have some issues with it. He snapped at the mention of Wonderland and didn't stop moving his mouth as if he were hissing.

"So what should I do?" Adrianna asked. "How do we get him to go back?"

"We have a mirror," Alice said with a smile, her mind going right to Wonderland. "All we need to do is convince him to go through and we're done! And then we can start looking for Evan's heart. I bet he put it in the walls here. The Queen put all the hearts behind glass walls and she had to have gotten that from somewhere, right?"

"Good idea," Adrianna said, taking a step back. She was already looking through the walls for something to float into view, but she left the flashlight off for now so Alice could do her work.

Around them, the surface of the glass, reflective in the dark, started to shift and change until they were surrounded by a familiar looking courtyard. Even Adrianna dimly remembered it from the time Cat threatened her last semester. Guards wandered around and flamingos aimlessly batted the balls around with their heads as if they knew that was what they were supposed to do but they couldn't think of why. Alice thought the Queen could use a visit from her old pet.

The Jabberwocky got up on the tip of its claws and skittered back from the walls of the cave, Alice and Adrianna moving to separate sides of the cave in order to get out of the way, and it shot a flame from its strange mouth at the walls. Alice twitched and felt something snap as the light of the flame made Wonderland vanish.

"I don't think he likes Wonderland," Adrianna said.

"But he's *from* Wonderland," Alice told her, looking back helplessly as the walls, still hot from the fire, were smoking and settling back down. At least now she knew why the whole inside of this place looked like glass. She also knew that this thing was definitely not as nice as Adrianna thought it was.

Alice thought for a moment, but found a new plan was easy to come up with. "Can you think of a way to keep it calm for a minute while I do that again?" Alice asked.

"I think so," Adrianna said. "Alice, what are you going to do?"

"Go over there," Alice said. "If I call it from that side, it should follow me in. Then I just have to jump back and we'll be looking for Evan in no time."

"You aren't going to get stuck over there, are you?"

Alice shook her head. "Not if I'm quick," she said. "Who's going to keep me there if I'm there for less than ten seconds?"

Adrianna seemed to take that as enough of an answer and turned her attention to the Jabberwocky, who was still silently hissing and screaming at the walls. Alice was glad she silenced it and wondered how long it would last.

Adrianna spoke to it in gentle, almost musical tones and it seemed to calm down. She managed to make it turn away from the walls altogether and look at the mouth of the cave, stroking it's head and keeping it calm.

Alice had to think of a place with a mirror so that she could get back. She could look in anywhere she wanted, but since the exit was always a mirror, she needed something shiny on the other side to get her back.

There was one place she hadn't been to before that might work. Wherever Cat was, whenever he looked at her it was always from the field of decapitated flowers and it probably had a huge mirror. It would have to do, even if it meant that she would have to run into him again. Maybe if she made it quick enough, maybe then it would be fine.

She thought of the field and it appeared before her. Looking at it now, she recognized it. It was where Alice had come out last semester and she didn't remember there being something huge and reflective there before. That is, until she noticed that there were a few flowers missed in whatever decapitated the rest of the field that seemed to be primping and gazing into the mirror longingly.

She would be quick. Talking flowers were not something she wanted to deal with.

She stepped through into Wonderland, finding it once again to be bright and a bit too warm for the coat she was wearing. Still, she kept her mind on the task at hand. Looking back, she couldn't really see the entire cave anymore, just bits and pieces of it from this side. She concentrated hard and was able to see the Jabberwocky with its back turned, looking content.

"*Ábedecian bealu gásric ælwiht hércyme,*" Alice said, looking straight at the Jabberwocky. It turned and looked like it was going to regret this. Still, it walked forward, one clawed step at a time, scratching at the floor as it did so. It was reluctant, but it was unable to help itself as she led it into Wonderland. It made every step carefully and eventually it was all the way through.

Alice breathed a sigh of relief. That was easy, though the Jabberwocky looked like it had just walked into a lion's den and it was nothing more than a small rabbit. It belonged here, though, so Alice didn't know what it was so upset about.

"Back home," Alice told it, trying to be reassuring as she stepped back a few more paces. All she needed now was for it to go running away from the mirror so that she could walk back through. It was strange that there was a mirror set up here in the middle of the field.

Slowly, the Jabberwocky drew forward, following Alice's careful steps backwards into Wonderland. She just needed to make sure it was in far enough that it wouldn't turn around again when she left and slip through before she could close the window from the other side. Just a little more.

It suddenly stopped and sat up straight, nose in the air and smelling something strange. Alice didn't like the look of it.

Behind him, the mirror dropped down to the ground and shattered against the rocks that propped it up. She stared at where the mirror used to be and the man who was standing there now. He wore a very large top hat and looked much more deranged than the last time she had seen him. He sat at a full table that she did recognize except for the lack of broken clocks.

The mirror had concealed the whole table of the tea party. The Dormouse was still asleep in the sugar bowl, though there were a few more faces she didn't recognize at the table as well, none of whom were drinking any tea.

A smug pair of eyes were on the table, followed soon afterwards by the grin, then the fur of the Cheshire Cat. She'd been set up.

"Why Alice," the Mad Hatter said, grinning too widely and too happily. "What a pleasure to have you join us for tea!"

CHAPTER 11

A Decent Proposal

ALICE WAS NOT happy at all to see them. The Jabberwocky kept her from joining them and she was tempted to try and convince it to distract them while she ran to find another mirror. She hoped that she could find another one and get out of here quickly, but luck was not on her side.

She turned to try and leave when she felt something on her shoulders. Something warm and with fur that needed a good brushing. The purple face appeared in front of her a moment later, grinning its wide grin and Alice was not happy. She ducked out of the floating cat's clutches and to the clock-covered place where the tea party used to be.

The Cheshire Cat's smiling grin followed her there. "Terribly rude of you to leave without so much as a hello!"

"I put the Jabberwocky back in Wonderland," she told him as she tried to make her flustered mind think of a mirror.

One that wasn't in the Queen of Heart's room of still beating hearts. There had to be another one in here somewhere. "It's done. Now I'm going home."

"You won't be going anywhere," the Cheshire Cat said. "There is only one way left out in all of Wonderland for you now."

Alice turned back to look at the Cat, the colour draining from her face. Her mind tried to come up with the image of a reflective surface somewhere. Anywhere. A glass surface in a dark place. A particularly calm body of water. Anything. "You can't have gotten all of them. There's got to be one."

"There's no ice to save you here. Not even the shoulders of Wonderland grow that cold. Now, won't you come back for some tea?"

Alice kept trying to find something reflective. The only thing that she could find, that she started moving towards before snapping herself out of it, was the mirror in the Queen's room of hearts and a few reflective bits here and there also in her castle. She couldn't find another one anywhere. She started walking, looking for anything, appearing and disappearing across Wonderland and looking frantically for anything that would show her a panicked looking Alice looking back.

Cat followed her with every step, but nothing looked back at her with her own face. There were people, but there were no mirrors anywhere and she realized that she was trapped.

"Come now, Alice," Cat said, still grinning cruelly as he followed behind her, then in front of her, then beside, then above, dropping down in front of her face so she stopped. "It is very rude to walk away from an invitation. I daresay you might have offended the Mad Hatter. Although, he may be a little busy with that friend you brought."

Alice struggled with herself before turning away and stepping back to the shards of broken mirror. They were all so tiny that she didn't think she could get a foot through one, much less the rest of her. She let out a sigh and tried to accept this as her fate. Wonderland wanted her back and Cat had made it happen. She hoped this wouldn't take too long.

Adrianna was still in the middle of the forest. Alice hoped that Adrianna could find her own way back and that she understood that Alice didn't mean for this to happen. She didn't know how far the Jabberwocky took them, but maybe it wouldn't be a difficult path to follow back. Just follow the trail of destruction back to the school.

She looked back at the tea party, surprised to find that the Jabberwocky hadn't taken flight and bolted yet. Instead, it sat obediently in front of the Mad Hatter and let him pat his scaly hide, though he was still uneasy about everything and everyone else around him.

Alice approached carefully, the Mad Hatter looking too distracted with this new creature to be bothered that Alice had vanished on him. Good enough for her. At least she wouldn't have to worry about that part of a lecture about manners as she came up to greet them. The Cat appeared back on the table, flicking the side of the sugar bowl and slamming the lid down on it to catch the Dormouse. It didn't work, the Dormouse rolling out of the sugar bowl and continued to roll until he was now sleeping in a tea cup.

Cat kept trying, but the Dormouse continued to wander about the table, rolling or walking lazy, half-sleeping steps. Behind them, there were two round boys who were talking to one another, looking angry about something though Alice didn't try to find out what. There was also an unfortunately familiar egg sitting at the far end of the table. He, thankfully, had not thought to look her way yet.

"What a delightful creature you've brought with you!" The Mad Hatter said, smiling wide as he patted the Jabberwocky.

The Jabberwocky still didn't like Alice; she could tell from how it watched her as she got closer and the dragon-like creature bared its sideways fangs at her when she dared to look at him for too long.

"He's something all right," Alice agreed.

"But terribly rude of you to show up with an unannounced guest!" The Hatter continued. "I do hope we can find the extra space and cups! Oh my, I think we have enough space. You will have to forgive Alice. Nice girl, but terribly rude. No manners at all."

Alice briefly wondered if the Jabberwocky would do her the kindness of eating her if she got close enough.

She took her seat at the table as far away from the Jabberwocky as she could manage, just as the Cheshire Cat seemed to want her to do. At least the Cat was amused by this. She hoped that Wonderland would give her some way out sooner rather than later. She was playing its game now. Or, at the very least, she was playing whatever game the Cheshire Cat wanted to play.

"Why, not even so much as an introduction," the Hatter continued.

"This is the Jabberwocky," Alice said. "Jabberwocky, this is the Mad Hatter."

"It isn't polite to be offering someone else's name without their bidding."

Alice put her jacket over the back of her chair, sat down and clenched her jaw shut. She wondered how bad it would have really been if she didn't bring the Jabberwocky back. A few more missing students? Some stolen hearts and empty kids wandering around the woods? She would have volunteered to be one of those empty beings right about now.

She managed to sit up straight and look ahead, not making any more noise or offering a single word. She would be quiet. If she was quiet, maybe everyone would forget she was here.

The Cheshire Cat smiled cruelly at her, mischief in his eyes. His tail flicked and he knocked over the cup behind him into the lap of Humpty Dumpty, who looked like he was missing a few pieces of shell since Alice saw him last.

"You," he said, both accusing and unimpressed. "The rude girl with the stupid name that was getting in my way. Didn't you get carted off by that terrible knight?"

Alice nodded, but tried not to say anything to keep the conversation continuing. Only answer exactly what they asked. Nothing more and much less if she could get away with it.

"Well?" Humpty Dumpty demanded. "Are you going to give me a proper greeting and tell me how you managed to escape that fiend? He left me shattered, you know. No horses or men to come to put me back together again, so I had to do it myself! The least you could have done was come back once you were done and helped return me to my full state again as an apology for how rude you were. I was lucky to get a little help from a few kind squirrels, but they were more interested in using me to store their nuts than actually rebuilding my poor shell."

If her one escape from Wonderland wasn't in the room of still beating hearts, Alice would have been gone. It didn't matter where. She would walk through fire and knives and anything else to get back home. It had to be in the room of hearts. And the Cheshire Cat wasn't going to let her get to a mirror any other way.

With Humpty Dumpty mercifully distracted by his now imperfect shell and the sound he made when he moved. Alice could hear the nuts rattling in his belly when he jiggled. She went back to staying still and waited until the next person decided that she was rude and wanted to tell her all about how it was terrible that she was such a rude girl. She could wait.

Across the table were the two round boys. Alice watched them for a moment, not quite hearing their conversation, but she managed to at least catch their names. Tweedle Dee and Tweedle Dum. They were probably the only people at the table that didn't find her rude yet. Maybe she could escape with just one of them not accusing her of being rude. Just one.

"Now that we're all here," The Cheshire Cat said, grinning wide at Alice, "perhaps we should consider beginning."

It sounded almost as if they had been waiting for her to join for a while. Alice looked down and saw that the legs of the table were covered in moss. Vines crawled along the surface. The snacks always looked inedible and the tea was always cold, but she wasn't sure why they would have set up for tea here this whole time.

She saw the way the Cat was looking at her and would not take the bait. He wanted her to ask.

Alice didn't want to know what the beginning was. She didn't want to know what was going on, but knew she would be brought into it whether she wanted to be or not. She would just be rude again if she said anything or tried to point out that they never asked her before forcing her into whatever shenanigans they had planned.

"Yes," the Mad Hatter said, clapping his hands together happily. "I didn't know if you were right, dear Cat, but you were right! We just needed to wait a little longer."

They really were waiting here this whole time for her, weren't they?

"I'm bored!" one of the pair said. Tweedle Dee.

"I'm more bored!" said the other.

"I assure you both that boredom is the least of your concerns," Humpty Dumpty said. "At least you have all your heads together, what parts of them actually work."

"Well, we might have gotten moving sooner if Alice weren't so late," the Mad Hatter said. Alice could barely contain her squeal of frustration and the Cheshire Cat was far too amused at her suffering for her liking. "Unfortunately, you know, girls run a bit slower so it might not quite be her fault. And she has brought us a delightful new companion."

While the Mad Hatter was happy about the Jabberwocky, the Jabberwocky was not happy about any of them. It stayed with only its back claws resting on the ground and nothing else, staying behind the Mad Hatter and with its wings almost fully unfurled in order to look as threatening as it could manage. Alice could count every one of its teeth if she were feeling daring, which she really was not. She could sympathize, though. These were the most annoying people that the Jabberwocky would ever encounter.

"Perhaps we should finish our tea," the Mad Hatter suggested, a grin creeping across his face. "It has been so long since we-"

"Why were you waiting for me?" Alice asked, remembering that look. Rude Alice could handle, but she wasn't about to start running around trying change places and potentially making the Jabberwocky even more anxious than he already looked.

"Why because you have a part to play, my dear!" The Mad Hatter said as if it were the most obvious thing in the world. "I daresay it is one of the most important parts of all."

"It is?" Alice was not looking forward to it. She was, in fact, already coming up with a list of ways to set the Cheshire Cat on fire in order to make him pay for bringing her back into this.

Alice already didn't like this. She ignored the looks of

everyone else and especially bypassed the Cheshire Cat when she looked down to the Dormouse, who rolled into her empty cup. "I'm awake," he said. "I wasn't sleeping. Just resting my eyes."

"Dormouse!" the Mad Hatter said. "Alice seems to have forgotten what's happened! Remind her, would you?"

"It started a very long time ago," he began. "Way back when the land was just learning to sing."

"Perhaps not that far back," Alice suggested. "Please. Just what we're doing now and what you would like me to do."

"Well, join us for tea," the Dormouse said. "What else would you be doing at a tea party?"

Alice hated the mouse as much as she hated everyone else here. "And what will we be doing after the party?" Alice asked, sounding sickeningly sweet to cover the depths of her loathing of everyone here. "A nice walk?"

"We're going to see the Queen," the Dormouse said. "The Queen quite likes you, you know. She would like a daughter and we would much like to offer you to her as that new daughter so that she might be happy enough to return the Hare and the White King to us."

Alice looked down at the Dormouse and tried to work through what he had just told her. They were going to be handing her over to the Queen in exchange for the White King and the Hare. She was being given as a sacrifice. They waited for her so long just so she could be their sacrifice? What if she never came?

"But what if I don't want to be the Queen's daughter?" she asked. "I am already my mother's daughter and I am quite happy there."

"Oh, Alice dear," The Cheshire Cat said, almost pitying her and with that spark in his eye that she didn't trust. He appeared once more over her shoulders and grinned wickedly. "But this is a queen. It is very rude to refuse the wishes of a queen. And besides, I've seen your mother and she is no queen. With the Queen of Hearts, you could become a princess. Isn't that what you want, Alice? To be a princess?"

Alice couldn't remember a time she ever wanted to be a princess. She could remember a time when she thought she was like a prisoner and times when she was actually a prisoner. She thought being the Queen of Heart's daughter would probably be a lot like that. Which, truth be told, was a bit like being her mother's daughter. Except that her mother didn't have a terrible room of hearts in their house.

"I think I'll pass," Alice said, trying to rise and finding that the Cheshire Cat would not move. It wasn't that he was pressing down on her shoulders. No, it was like he was now a shelf that had appeared over her that she could not move out from under. Try though she might to get up, he was there, trapping her down on the chair. His tail curled around her neck and he stretched down her arm to rest on it, keeping her quite solidly in place.

She looked at the Jabberwocky, knowing that the creature was uncomfortable and trying to think of a way out of what was happening. The Jabberwocky was still silent, but she hoped it would be able to yell soon. Maybe she could keep herself together for one of its screams so that she could run for it.

Alice tried to get back up again, but she couldn't get out from under the Cat. The Mad Hatter seemed to be oblivious to her distress, along with everyone else. They all seemed to think this was a fantastic idea and Alice would be happy as the new princess of Wonderland.

"Oh, it will be so much fun to have a Princess around," the Mad Hatter said, sounding like this was the best thing to happen to him in a very long time. "And it will be good to have that Hare back as well. March Hare he may be, but he has not been doing his fair share of the marching of late. Taking a break in the castle! He will be making it up to me!"

"You know he's not quite the same anymore, right?" Alice asked. She looked for something - anything - to stall until she came up with some better idea. "He's going to be just a shell of what he once was."

The Cat twitched on her shoulders. The Mad Hatter looked at her and was quite curious. "Well, that might just be a fantastic thing!" he said, the bright side seeming to come far too easily to him. "I always thought he needed to be filled with something a bit different. His thoughts were always thinking and that did not bode well for him, as you well know. I shall know better what to fill him with, though, and it will be so good to work with a blank slate."

"The king too!" Alice said, trying to keep him talking. Maybe he could be worried enough about this that he'd rethink the idea. Maybe he would just think long enough that he could maybe manage to find something else to do instead. Or he'd get bored and let Alice go so he could torment someone else with tea.

"Well that isn't quite as good," the Mad Hatter said. "We will need to fill him back up with all his royalness that he should be filled with. Royal thoughts and royal actions and I do not have many of those things. Perhaps we all have enough together. We can find another King to fill him up with."

"I know how to be royal!" Tweedle Dee said. "It's all about waving and telling people what to do!"

"No, it's about moving your hands right and being in perfect command!"

Alice watched as the twins devolved into an argument about which of their two slightly differently phrased statements was correct. The Cat moved around her shoulders until he was glaring back at her. She knew what he was trying to say. He thought that she should stop trying and accept her fate already. That was not about to happen.

Alice saw Humpty Dumpty get involved in the argument, saying that he was clearly the most qualified person to talk about royalness, as he knew the King for the longest and would be able to most accurately remind the King what it was he was supposed to be.

"There's something else you could do," Alice said, seeing the Jabberwocky starting to move its mouth again. She couldn't hear it over the sound of everything else, but the flaps on the side of its head fluttered. It could hear something and it wasn't scared of it. Only a little time left now, she hoped, before his voice would come back. "If the Queen took their hearts, which is what she's doing to everyone then all you need to do is-"

Fur filled her mouth as the Cheshire Cat put his tail between her teeth. She sputtered around it, but he did not move from keeping it firmly in there to shut her up. She couldn't say anything more, but she could feel the low rumbling growl from the Cat all the way though her arm and in her mouth, the displeasure spreading through his whole body. He was not pleased with her.

"Now come on everyone," the Mad Hatter said, trying to bring order to his table. "Calm down. This is a civil event. Tea parties are meant to be lovely gatherings and we do not fight."

"Perhaps you should head along ahead," the Cheshire Cat said. "You should be there to greet the Queen on time. Not too early and not too late. Punctuality is important for royalty. If it weren't, why would the words rhyme so well?"

"You are quite right!" the Mad Hatter said. "Come along now, we must be going. We shall need to see the Queen about letting us see a few friends again."

CHAPTER 12

Reasonable Exchange

WHILE EVERYONE ELSE got up and went off to see the queen with a spring in their step, Alice remained stuck to the chair, pinned by the Cheshire Cat and unable to leave no matter how much she tried.

With his tail in her mouth and claws in her arm, Alice tried to kick the chair out from under her to get out of his clutches. Even with it gone, she dangled in the air, suspended by the Cheshire Cat. She couldn't move and couldn't find another place to step to, though she tried.

"After all that trouble, I don't think you'll be escaping this particular predicament," the Cheshire Cat said, grinning up at her again.

Alice tried to make a sound, but Cat shushed her, smiling at her pityingly. "Now Alice, this is not the way a young girl should behave. Perhaps it's best if you rethink your actions.

You could be a princess. You will have power and you will have a mother who is available. One who likely won't keep a key to your room in her pocket all day. The Queen will love you much more than that other mother of yours. Why, look at what yours did to her daughters."

Alice stopped struggling at that, wondering what the Cat knew that she didn't. Did he know something about Lori? No, that was just him pretending that he knew more than he did. Maybe he learned something, but chances were that he knew nothing more than she did. Lori was off somewhere, and their mother wouldn't have gotten rid of her, just like she'd never get rid of Alice.

"One sent away. Another one sent to her room so often it might as well be a prison. She locks you away in there when you are bad, or locks you away in the house when you are good. You already have the same amount of freedom as a princess. The difference is that your new house will be far bigger and give you more space to roam. You will be able to explore freely without breaking into rooms you should not be in. You will have people around all day who will speak to you and who will play with you and who will not try to forget you. People who will believe everything you have to say about Wonderland. Now, be a good girl and stay."

He removed his tail, but not his claws. Alice tried to spit out the fur that remained in her mouth, but the furry feeling of the tail in there would not leave. She would have to deal with that for a while, she figured. At least there was no more tail in her mouth.

She looked flatly back down at the Cat's expectant eyes. "You want to go back over," she said. "You want me to let you go back over to my world so you can escape the Queen, don't you? You did all this just so you could make me let you go back."

"Why Alice, dear," he said, kneading into her arm more, Alice wincing as his claws tore into her skin. She thought there would be blood when she looked again. "You have such a low opinion of me. I am only thinking of what would be the very best for you."

"Or what's best for you," Alice said. "What else did you do here? Do they know you're giving them all over to the Queen of Hearts? And giving her back her heart thief?"

"Returning the Jabberwocky is your fault, Alice," Cat said. "I was not the one who brought it. I would not have brought it back at all. It was content in the forest outside your school, simply watching and eating the Jubjub birds and chasing the students that ventured too far in. I would have left him there, not brought him back to where he might be made to cause even more mischief."

"He's *from* here," Alice said. "He doesn't belong out in my woods. He belongs in yours."

"You presume too much, Alice dear," he said. "What did you learn of the book? It appeared in Wonderland from the sky, striking down a king. Does that sound like something Wonderland would do?"

Alice didn't care. She was more concerned with being stuck in Wonderland and becoming the Queen's daughter. She worried she wouldn't be able to escape before her heart was ripped from her chest. There was something special about the fear that she was going to lose her heart that made it very difficult for Alice to think of places to run to.

Alice said nothing more and stopped struggling. She was tired. She had run through the woods already and now she was about to do this. She was doomed. Completely doomed. She just wanted to go back home and make sure Adrianna found her way back as well.

"Come now," the Cat said, slipping his tail back over her face and covering her eyes. "We mustn't be late for your time with the Queen. I do wish you had chosen something nicer to wear, though. That outfit is nothing to see royalty in. She will likely be quite offended and might not even take you. And if she is, then this may fare poorly for everyone else. It would be to your best interests if you were to behave yourself to ensure no one else suffers for your rudeness. You do have quite the problem with that. But worry not. We have just the solution for that."

Cat stuck his claws deep into Alice's arm and she let out a yelp of pain. Cat stuck his large tail back in her mouth, silencing her and his tail fluffed up to cover the rest of her face.

A moment later, she knew they were no longer at the tea party. Alice could hear people talking about the lovely young present that they had brought and how it was going to make the Queen so very happy to see. Alice knew they were all talking about her. They were all smiling — she could hear it in the sneering words — but they also seemed to be keeping their distance. There was something about the whole thing that felt off.

When Cat finally let the puff of his tail settle, Alice could see why it was so quiet.

They were in the throne room, standing in front of the Queen of Hearts with the Mad Hatter bowing low and trying to smile as best he could.

"What makes you think I will not take your hearts and add them to my collection?" the Queen asked, stepping toward them all and bending down to stroke under the Mad Hatter's chin. He looked up at her beckoning, though he was still grinning madly.

"We come with a gift," he said simply. "We know how much you wanted a pretty daughter. There was one that the Cheshire Cat said that you had your eye on and we've brought her here." He stood and moved with a flourish, getting out of the way to let the Queen see Alice there, pinned to the chair by the Cheshire Cat.

The Queen regarded Alice and Alice glared back at her, Cat preventing her from speaking as she struggled anew. The Queen did not look impressed. "You bring me this?" she demanded, looking over Alice unpleasantly. "She looks far too unruly to be anything that I would ever be interested in. I see your game is to waste my time. What makes you think I shouldn't rip out your hearts for my collection right now?"

"Why, because we've brought you precisely what you wanted," the Mad Hatter said, though he faltered. Alice could hear the tinge of panic in his voice and she struggled even harder to try and get out. The Cat sunk his claws in deeper and hissed back up at her in a warning that she understood. If she misbehaved, the Queen would make them suffer.

"Perhaps another look, your majesty," the Cheshire Cat suggested. "You understand, she may have looked unruly in the light. Over here might be a bit better."

Cat moved them to by the throne, to where a princess might sit at the hand of the Queen. She was not comfortable here, but Alice saw no choice left to her but to obey for now. She had to do something. And by something, she would do nothing, sitting perfectly still and taking in the rest of the room around the Queen as she approached for a better look.

Tweedle Dee and Tweedle Dum looked like they'd seen

better days, already beaten and detained by the guards, who held them each back from interfering again. Alice liked them more already. Behind them, the Jabberwocky was kept down with several ropes and chains, keeping him on the ground and out of any trouble. She could hear the soft growling coming out of him.

His voice was back.

Her idea was simple. She just needed to get something to annoy the Jabberwocky enough to set it loose and she could get out of there. She could do this. She had to. Now, what would piss off the Jabberwocky enough to make it scream?

And how was she going to get Cat off of her?

"Well, I suppose she is nice enough," the Queen said, looking close and grabbing her chin. She looked over her hair and her skin, seeing that her arm was damaged, she clicked her tongue in disapproval, as well as at the tears in her pants and the scratches beneath them. She was not a fully satisfactory package, to be sure, but the Queen seemed to think it was something she could work with.

"She is a bit plain," the Queen said, studying her carefully. "I suppose she will do, though."

"Then we can discuss payment," the Mad Hatter said.

"Payment?" the Queen sounded that sort of amused that meant that everyone should run, but the Mad Hatter didn't seem to realize that as he continued to smile. Alice noticed he had another hat in his hand and he put that back on top of his smaller top hat that was still on his head.

"Of course!" Hatter said. "In exchange for Alice, I would very much like the return of the March Hare and the White King. We have quite missed them, you see, and would like to see them again. We will give you Alice for both of them."

"I will take the girl," the Queen said, turning on him and looking livid. "I was considering letting *one* of you leave with your heart still intact so that you could provide a bit of fun, but for such assumptions and attempting to make your queen pay for a gift, you shall receive no such fairness and grace."

Alice did the only thing she could and let out a desperate cry, her muffled yelp around the Cat's tail just distracting enough that the Queen hesitated, looking back to see what that noise was. Alice kept struggling against Cat, trying to twist out of there.

It was enough, though it wasn't Alice's plan to have it happen this way. The Jabberwocky could clearly see that the Queen was about to do something to the Hatter, who he actually seemed to like. The Queen's moment of distraction was enough for the Jabberwocky to rear up onto his hind legs, breaking out of the chains and ropes and people holding him down. He let out a large roar that shook the air around them. His clawed wings extended in full, tearing through the tapestries as he blew out a mighty flame.

Alice felt Cat claw even deeper into her arm as the Jab-berwocky set his eyes in front of him. Alice didn't know who he was looking at, either her or the Queen or maybe even Cat, before he charged forward. With one pace, it cleared the room and the Cheshire Cat jumped off her shoulders into mid-air and vanishing from sight.

Alice left after him, nothing else in her mind but getting out of there before the Jabberwocky had a chance to do any-thing else. She ended up just outside the throne room, that apparently being as far as "out" would take her.

She ran through the halls as the screeching of the Queen filled the air. The Queen didn't sound like she was being eaten or burned alive, instead calling for reinforcements that came in droves. They bypassed Alice completely, who stayed out of their way and looked at the deep scratches left in her arms by Cat.

While she was tempted to go back and make sure that the Hatter was all right, she reminded herself that he had just tried to sell her. She wasn't going to stick around while the Jabberwocky terrorized the castle. She could already see the flames erupting from the throne room where it was currently running out of things to set on fire.

Still, Alice hesitated. There was one way she knew of back home, but she didn't want to go there. On the other hand, there was a dragon running down the hall after her and she really didn't want to be caught in that. Behind her, she saw that the Mad Hatter and the twins were running behind the Jabberwocky instead of in front of it, so Alice figured they would be fine.

They could still get a little singed, though. It wouldn't be that bad to see them at the very least singed for their troubles.

She could keep her eyes closed, she decided. Maybe if she could just ignore the hearts or think of them as wallpaper. If they were just ugly wallpaper, she could do that. And she really didn't want to get eaten by an angry dragon. She could do this. It was her only way out.

A few steps later, her feet hit glass and she kept her eyes closed. She could hear the beating hearts pounding all around her and she knew she was in the right place. She tried to keep her panic down, but no amount of deep breaths or imaginations could convince her that it was only wallpaper.

She was here with a goal. All she needed to do was get to the mirror.

Alice opened her eyes and was grateful to see the mirror was right in front of her. She was considerably less grateful to see perched atop it was a large purple cat that had every hair standing on edge. He did not look happy to be in here either.

"Hello, Alice," he said, his voice even sounding grating in this room.

"Move," she said.

"That's not very—"

"Get out of my way you stupid cat!" she yelled at it.

"Well aren't we rude."

He stretched out over the surface of the mirror as Alice tried to see her dorm room through the reflection. With Cat blocking it, she couldn't see much, but she hoped it would be there on the other side when she finally got rid of him.

He tried to smile, but the beating of the room unsettled him as much as Alice. "I always hated this place," he said, his eyes going to the hearts. Alice desperately tried not to look at them, instead focusing on the bits of her dorm room and trying to imagine Adrianna's music over the beating hearts. In her mind, they were becoming the same, the beating of the hearts the same as the beats of the music. "It's much too loud."

"Get out!" Alice yelled at him. She tried to grab him. He took a swipe at her and scratched the palm of her hand, making her recoil back in pain.

Cat hissed at her and glared at her with all the maliciousness he could muster. "You know what I want," he said. "If you let me through, I will let you go. If not, this mirror will meet the same fate as all the rest."

"You!"

Alice snapped around. She was ready to give him what he wanted, but the Queen of Hearts demanded her attention more. She had clearly been caught in the flame. Her dress was scorched and her hair on fire, but that was hardly the end of it. It was like she was melting, her skin still bubbling though she didn't seem to feel any pain from it. She looked at Alice like she was ready to take her skin to replace the parts of her own that had melted away, which was a lot. Alice, if she had been able to think straight, would have wondered how her eye stayed in the socket with so little left to support it.

All around her, Alice could still hear the hearts beating. Her own heart pounded the loudest.

"You come here, child," she said in a manner that made Alice want to do no such thing. Her voice was high, raspy and like her lungs were about to burst forth with a bright stream of flame. Alice couldn't even bring herself to back away, frozen as her mind went white with fear.

"Well, that's unexpected," Cat said, as if to assure her that not only was he still there, but he also wasn't nearly as terrified of this as she was. Alice knew she needed to leave, but she couldn't move or even remember anything else existing outside of this room with the Queen advancing on her.

"Come here," the Queen commanded. "I am your Queen and I demand your heart, child. If you give me your heart, I will make you my daughter. I will make you a pretty little thing for others to behold and you will do what I say. Now give me your heart."

Something in Alice snapped as the Queen took a step closer. Her body moved on its own.

She reached back to where the Cheshire Cat started to slink up behind the mirror, tail straight up in the air. She grabbed him by the tail, catching him completely by surprise, and flung him at the Queen of Hearts. The Queen took Cat in the face, the Cheshire Cat panicking and clawing at her before disappearing into the air.

Alice dove straight through the mirror. She breathed heavily and realized there were tears streaming down her face. A moment later, the image of the Queen still burned into her mind, she ran into the washroom and proceeded to empty her stomach of anything that was left in there. After it was empty, she continued to retch into the bowl, dry heaving and tears mingling together.

"I don't think Alice is feeling well," she heard from the door of the dorm room. Alice didn't get up.

"Maybe next time, then," a voice said. Sarah. "Maybe if she's okay, you guys could still come out."

"Maybe," Adrianna said, closing the door behind her and heading to the bathroom.

Alice didn't move, still lying on the toilet bowl and wanting to curl up here for a few days. Maybe a week. Just until she could get that image out of her mind. As if the pounding hearts weren't bad enough, now she was going to be having nightmares about a melting Queen of Hearts.

"Alice?" Adrianna asked. "Are you okay?"

"I think so," Alice said, letting Adrianna help her get shakily back to her feet and get her a glass of water. She forced herself to breathe and calm down, pushing every image she could out of her mind. She didn't need to think about it anymore. She was safe here in the dorm. None of it was real here.

She needed something else to focus on.

Adrianna was fine, thankfully, and had gotten back to the dorm without her. She was also not wearing the same thing as she was earlier. "I'm sorry," Alice said. "I didn't think... I didn't mean to leave you there. I didn't mean to go. I didn't want to go. I never want to go."

"It's okay," Adrianna said. "You're back now. And it wasn't that far. The Jabberwocky's cave was just a little way in the woods."

"How long was I gone?" Alice asked.

"Only a day this time. It's Sunday night."

"Oh good."

"What happened?"

"I think I need a little bit before I tell you about it."

"But it's over, right? No more Jabberwocky?"

A smile crept over Alice's face. "No more Jabberwocky."

CHAPTER 13

Not Quite Over

A WEEK PASSED with absolutely nothing out of the ordinary happening. Alice fell into her usual life, one that didn't involve any of Wonderland or wandering through the woods. She went to classes, did homework, and hung out with her friends. It was fantastic.

Not even a single person heard the ghost. It was gone now that the Jabberwocky was back in Wonderland. There was talk of something strange moving in the woods, but no one was concerned about it anymore. Some people thought it was the victims of the ghost moving through the woods, but most let the matter drop entirely.

Adrianna forgot about Evan every night. After a few days of having the same conversation with her about her brother, convincing her with almost no trouble, only to have her forget again a day later, Alice let the subject drop. She could just work on getting her brother back. Once Evan was back, this Jabberwocky nonsense would be over for good.

Alice had gone back to the cave a few times with a flashlight to try and find the hearts. It was, honestly, an unenthusiastic effort. She didn't actually want to find any hearts in the walls, floating there and still beating. Still, there was a missing brother and, while they literally had so many that one had gone missing without anyone noticing, she still felt responsible.

She also didn't know who else might be missing.

What was she going to do once she found Evan and his heart? She couldn't just put it back, could she? Maybe it would be as simple as handing it to Evan and he'd be able to put it back in himself. She hoped that he didn't have some huge hole in his chest. She had already dealt with a melting Queen. She didn't need to deal with someone with a hole in their chest the size of a claw and a bloody, beating heart as well.

On the bright side, there was a break coming up. With two weeks off for Spring Break, most people were going to leave campus. She would be able to look for everyone and everything then without anyone wondering where she went.

Near the end of the week, Sarah booked the movie room in the dorms so that she could force everyone into taking a night off. They popped in a movie and celebrated mostly by relaxing with one of many movies that Alice had never seen before. Robert was appalled that she hadn't even heard of either *Star Wars* or *Star Trek*, while there were movies from *The Breakfast Club* to *Legally Blonde* that Heather insisted that they had to catch her up on. Adrianna suggested a few animated features and Alice was left to choose.

Alice settled on *Back to the Future*. It seemed like fun and no one really objected to it, though Sarah looked like she would have preferred *Legally Blonde*. Given that neither Kevin nor Robert were that keen on sitting through something that looked quite pink, she promised that they could watch it later without the boys.

"I am leaving all of these with you over Spring Break," Robert said, handing her a whole stack of DVDs with various fantasy and science fiction covers on them. "I don't know how you got by without having seen any of them. Even Sarah has seen them!"

"That's just because my brother is obsessed," Sarah said, rolling her eyes and crossing her arms. She had a younger brother that was still a bit too young to start school with them. Not that Sarah was unversed in the entire stack of movies. She leaned over to help go through some of the discs and stopped at one particular box set. "I'll join you for this one, though," she said. "*Lord of the Rings* is way better."

"Yeah, I could do a *Lord of the Rings* marathon. Oh, want

to do it after exams?" Heather suggested. "Nine hours of extended editions."

Robert looked distrustful of this enthusiasm, but they all agreed to it on the condition that they could swing one of the movie rooms. In the meantime, they only had time for one *Back to the Future* movie before curfew would ensure they were sent back to their dorms.

Robert and Sarah were volunteered to go get some snacks from the cafeteria when the movie started, Kevin insisting that Robert join Sarah when she offered. "He will quote every single line," Kevin told them when they left. "And trivia. Trust me, you don't want him here at the start of a movie."

Alice laughed and settled in to enjoy the adventures of Marty McFly, which seemed like a strange name, and a mad scientist that figured out how to time travel using a car. It was exactly the sort of film that her parents would have never let her watch, too filled with fantastic ideas she might believe, and she loved it. It was like Lori kept saying. Alice knew it wasn't real. It was just a little fun.

Snacks arrived with a few more bodies who settled in the back. Alice didn't pay attention, too amused at the moment that Marty accidentally made an impression on his mother and possibly messed up the timeline. Robert would occasion- ally point out something in the movie, which was met with a friendly smack from Kevin to shut the hell up.

Not that they didn't talk through the movie. Heather was more than happy to talk back when Robert pointed out something or to heckle various stupid decisions made by the characters. Even Alice ended up joining in, though her additions were usually questions that were answered with, "That's how these movies go," which was fine by her. The three similar voices in the back, Adrianna's brothers, ended up laughing the loudest when anything particularly clever was said, at one point giving Heather a round of applause.

It was over too soon and Alice was a bit sad that they wouldn't be able to watch the next one. They brought the lights up and gathered around what was left of the snacks.

"Why are you guys here?" Heather asked, looking between Adrianna's identical brothers, then glancing at Alice and Adrianna, unable to figure out which one was which. Thankfully, they were dressed differently today and they would be a bit easier to keep track of once they figured it out.

"We can't come celebrate Alice's birthday?" they asked, trying and failing to sound innocent. "Happy birthday Alice! You're how old now?"

Alice gave them a long look. "My birthday isn't for another two months," she said. "And I'm already old enough to know there's something else." She could tell which one was which, even without checking for their tells.

Matt laughed and cracked first. "We may also need an

alibi," he said. "If we're here, then no one's going to try saying we did anything else."

"And you came here because...?"

"So suspicious, Alice," Mark said, grinning. "You guys seem like good kids. I think we can tell you about it. See, tomorrow there's this big exam. It got sprung on us today and most of our class is currently studying like crazy. They wanted us to make sure the test didn't happen. They needed more time."

"And we don't want to get in trouble again," Mike chimed in. "Not for this one. We don't have a way to weasel our way out of it and no one to get us out of anything worse than maybe an in school suspension. So we refused and let them go ahead with all their studying and told them that if they wanted to stop the test so badly, then they would just have to do it themselves."

"And now they are," Matt said, rolling his eyes and sounding very unimpressed. "And you know they're going to try and pin the whole thing on us."

"Shouldn't you be studying, then?" Adrianna asked.

"Like we study," Mike said, laughing. "It'll be fine. Better to take the test well rested and relaxed after spending some time with our dear sister and her friends. All of whom are going to let the authorities know that we were here for the whole night."

He gave them all a meaningful and slightly threaten-ing look.

"Isn't there a camera in the hall?" Robert asked, pointing out into the hall behind the frosted glass back wall. "There's evidence without any of us."

"Do you know how easy it is to screw with those cam-eras?" Mike asked flatly. "They don't even have them secured. No, we need people to back up the footage. And so they knew we didn't go through the floor again."

"What?"

Mark hit one of the floor tiles hard with his heel and picked it up to reveal the space beneath the floor, all filled with a mess of wires and metal beams to secure everything in place. It was big enough down there that they could easily crawl through, and they might even be able to sit comfortably in some spots. He dropped the tile back down now that they had the idea.

"They still don't know how we did that one," Mike said, grinning to himself.

"So wait, you hacked into the school's network?"

"Guessing passwords is not hacking," Mike corrected him. "It's just luck. And it's not like we're screwing with grades or anything while we're in there. We're just covering our tracks once in a while. No harm."

"How are you not expelled?"

"Do you have access to student files?" Alice asked, the whole thing triggering something in the back of her mind. She felt the eyes on her immediately and she shrunk away from them. "Not that I'm asking you to do anything with them. I'm not."

"We might," Mark said, sliding in around Alice. "It depends on what you're looking for."

"Maybe to find out where your friend Cat went after last semester?"

"No," Alice said quickly, disgusted at the thought. She was glad to have gotten rid of him. "No, I just remember hearing there was someone named Evan who is supposed to go here. I think he was a bit older than Lori. She used to mention him when she was home, but no one's heard of him."

"The missing sister? I think we can look him up for you," Mike said. "Consider it an early birthday present."

"You sure he's real?" Mark asked. "If no one's heard of him, maybe she was talking to one of the campus ghosts."

"Again with the ghosts?" Kevin demanded. "It's been a whole week since I've heard about ghosts."

"They're not attacking students anymore," Matt told him. "Someone's herding them all into the forest. Some people are saying they're being called back there, but some people are starting to see them wandering around between the trees late at night. They look like students, ones that have been all killed on campus before. Those screams from before, they were the cries as those ghosts were trying to get away from whatever was after them, but now they're all being pulled back into the depths of the forest."

Alice fell quiet. People in the forest. If that were true, one of those people was probably Evan. And if they were coming out at night, it couldn't be that difficult to track them down. She did wonder what they were doing out at night, though. It was strange that they would be sleeping during the day and wandering around the forest at night, but Alice would take it.

"That is the stupidest thing I have ever heard," Kevin told them.

"I think that's how the Red Bull got all the unicorns in *The Last Unicorn*," Robert said. "Except with the tides instead of the forest."

"It's not perfect yet," Matt admitted. "We're still working on the story. But there are people walking around the forest at night. We think the seniors are doing some night class or something. And without the ghost around scaring people, we're running out of stuff to do that's not going to get us kicked out."

"You have a huge exam tomorrow and you're *bored*?"

"Pretty much."

"Teach me."

Alice looked around, suddenly aware that one of their

number was missing since the start of the movie. Adrianna, three brothers, Heather, Kevin and Robert were all here, but the bubbly blonde who had promised to set her up on a date next year was missing. She looked around, thinking maybe she'd just been sitting in one of the chairs or looking through the DVDs for something else to watch if they had time, but Alice didn't see any sign of her anywhere.

"Hey?" Alice asked, still searching for some sign of her. "Where's Sarah?"

Heather looked at her. "Who?"

CHAPTER 14

Not Completely Lost

THE BREAK WENT poorly for her. Alice was alone, Adrianna having gone home with her family to do whatever families did on breaks. That part wasn't so bad. She managed to watch several of the DVDs that Robert and Heather left her and started to learn about all the pop culture that she apparently desperately needed to know. If nothing else, she might be able to follow when they made references now.

No, her break was miserable for another reason altogether. Getting rid of the Jabberwocky hadn't solved anything, it seemed. The Jabberwocky was safely away in Wonderland, well away from where anyone could be taken by it, and Sarah still vanished. She went for snacks and not even the memory of her returned from the trip. Alice worried that the Jabberwocky managed to slip back onto campus again, but she went back to the cave and there was no sign of it.

She spent time every day and night looking for Evan's or Sarah's hearts in the Jabberwocky's cave walls and was a little relieved that she never found them. One the one hand, she desperately wanted to find them so that she could return everything to normal. On the other, she didn't know how to get them out of the wall if she did find them, or how to put the hearts back into them, or if that would solve anything.

There were also no people to find wandering the woods late at night. It probably was actually a class, now home for the holidays instead of wandering late at night for her to find. Even if she found Evan or Sarah out there, she would just have a person that no one could remember wandering behind her and it would be impossible to explain without sounding crazy.

And she didn't have their hearts.

When everyone came back two weeks later, it was April and Alice had just about given up. She was almost out of ideas. There had to be another place that the Jabberwocky could have hidden the hearts or that the people could be, but she drew a blank. There was also no other Jabberwocky according to the one page in the book on it, so she had no ideas as to how Sarah went missing.

She went back to classes when they resumed and kept her head down. She decided not to say anything about any of it to Adrianna or anyone else. Heather looked like she was enjoying her single room and, from what Alice could tell, all traces of Sarah were gone. It was like she'd never been there at all.

"Hey, Alice!"

Classes were just finishing for the day, Adrianna having to run off to choir and leaving Alice on her own. Alice was heading towards her locker and she looked back to see two of Adrianna's brothers approaching. It was eerie how similar they looked. They even carried themselves the same.

Which meant that she knew exactly which two these were.

"Hey," she said, dropping her bag and opening her locker to exchange her books. "What's up?"

"We need to have a little talk about that thing you asked us to look up a little while ago," Mark said, leaning against her open locker door.

"Are you sure this Evan guy was really a friend of your sister's?" Mike asked.

Alice could feel both of their eyes on her, but she did not to react. So they'd found something that they weren't happy with? Alice wasn't sure if she should be happy about it or not. She didn't even think they would be looking him up at all, but they found something on him. So he wasn't completely gone.

"We're thinking she didn't know this Evan guy at all," Mark pressed.

"So you found him?" Alice asked, closing her backpack and putting it back on.

"You could say that. You want to know what we found?"

She turned to look at Mark. "I'm curious," she admitted.

"You didn't think we'd find anything, did you?" Mike said behind her. Mark closed her locker for her. Alice stayed quiet so Mike continued. "If you want to know what we found out, our dorm room, eight tonight. Don't be seen."

"I don't even know where your dorm room is."

"And yet you managed to steal something out of there before," Mike said, waving goodbye with a small orange water gun in hand as he and Mark left.

"Addie knows if you don't," Mark added and they disappeared into the shuffling student body.

Alice watched them go, wondering what they might have found. She was going to try the book again tonight, just to see if maybe somewhere in that huge brown tome there was something in there about what to do with the hearts that were taken out of people and places that the Jabberwocky might have hidden them now that they were gone.

Still, it was curious. They might have found a trace of Evan left behind. Sarah's room was completely vacant, but there was a set of makeup she'd given to Heather that was still there. She wasn't completely erased, just mostly so. She hoped that meant that the missing people still existed somewhere.

Even if they did, she still didn't know where to find them.

And if she did find them, she didn't know how to get their hearts back in so that they would be remembered again.

If that was how that even worked.

Cat might know something. He always pretended to, at least. Maybe he knew how to put the hearts back in the people's chests and return them to who they once were. If the book didn't have any answers, she might have to try him. If she could find the people again.

When the clock struck eight, Adrianna was still not back from choir. A quick question around the dorms told her that choir was doing something to help the play for the end of the year, so they had double practices tonight, both for themselves and for the play.

Alice was at a loss. Mike and Mark's room was somewhere in this building in their year's wing on the boy's side. She hadn't even been to that section of the dorms, much less to the boy's side of them, so she wasn't sure where to start with getting there.

Then she remembered the water gun. She wrapped her mind around the water gun and reached forward for it, her hand hitting the pillow.

The rest of her appeared soon afterwards, sitting on a bed in a room that smelled very strongly of Doritos. It was set up much like Alice and Adrianna's room, with the two sides split down the middle. There were books on the beds and things on the walls that looked like they might fall down at any moment. Post-it notes covered the dressers, small reminders or ideas for later or maybe passive-aggressive notes for the other brother when one left something behind. It wasn't that messy, but it was clear that cleanliness was not their priority in here. Instead, it seemed to be much more about getting things done, as there were bits of wire and boxes of other things in here, as well as computers set up on either side of the room that looked much heavier duty than the laptop in Joe's room.

"Either someone's pulling a huge trick on us or she knows a lot more than she's letting on," Mike said, huddled around the computer. At his side, Mark was taking a look at whatever was on the screen and shaking his head. "You think they got Ryan in on it?"

"If she did, that's impressive," Mark said. He glanced at the door. "Alice better not bring Addie with her. I have no way to explain this one."

"Addie probably already knows everything," Mike said. "Chances are whatever Alice did here, or whoever got Alice into it, they couldn't keep her out. Still, Addie keeping her mouth shut this long is something I never thought I'd see."

"She keeps my secrets pretty well so far," Alice said. The two of them jumped and spun around to find her sitting on the bed, staring back at them. They looked between her and the door, their eyebrows knitting in concentration and they looked at her with a lot of distrust.

"When did you get here?" Mark asked, straightening up and getting closer to look her over. "And how did you get in here?"

"I walked," Alice said, meeting his eyes. The reality of it would make them think she was crazy and she really didn't want to have to deal with the ramifications of that.

"Through the door?"

"How else would I get in?"

Mark glanced up at the ceiling and Mike over at the washroom door, but neither said anything. Instead they exchanged a look and seemed to want to get down to business.

"One day we're going to figure out what's with you," Mark said, waving her over to the three monitor setup that Mike had in front of him. There were things on all the screens that Alice didn't know what to make of. There was a video on one, email on another and a lot of open files scattered across it, all in small windows nestled on the screen. "We just got an email from Ryan," Mark told her. "Decided to ask him about this Evan guy, but he's never heard of him either."

"Ryan is your oldest brother, right?" Alice asked.

"We found your Evan," Mike said, making a few of the windows bigger and spreading them across the monitors. There were pages of text with bits of them highlighted, documents and screen captures of something else she didn't know. It was impressive to say the least. "At least, *an* Evan. Evan Case."

"Yes, that's his name," Alice said, trying to keep her expression neutral as she looked across the screens. She couldn't quite grasp how he was able to go between them all without being distracted by something on another one. Worse were the nested windows on the last one. There were so many screens and Alice didn't know what she was supposed to be paying attention to.

"Interesting how he has no file anywhere, but he's been referenced several times over. Positive comments from teachers. Ran for Student Council roles for several years. Last seen applying and running for Treasurer and beating out some girl for it, and he was supposed to be taking up the position this year. But again, no file and this is just from an article in a paper I didn't know our school even had."

"Disbanded last year," Mark said. "No one was reading it and they didn't bother bringing it back this year."

"It's weird, though," Mike continued. "You'd think someone would have heard of another Case kid at this school. There's a lot of us, you know."

"Maybe it's a common last name," Alice suggested. "It's not that rare. There might be more than just your family."

"That is, until we found the pictures," Mark said, reaching over and taking the mouse from Mike. He brought up a couple photographs from years previous. Yearbook photos and school paper shots from a now defunct and vanished website with a Way Back Machine logo at the top of the page were brought up one by one and he started pointing them out. "There's this guy in all the pictures. Evan Case."

Evan was never at the center of the photo or the focus. There were a few where it looked like there should be someone else there, but there was no one. In the group shots and the ones where he was in the background, Evan Case smiled back very clearly.

"He looks awfully familiar, don't you think?"

Alice was glad there was still evidence that he used to be a student and that he once existed. It was comforting to know there was proof of him. Maybe she could get it printed out and give Adrianna a picture to keep with her so that it would help her remember him for longer than a day. Maybe her memory of him would come back for good after looking at him for a while.

"What do you know, Alice?" Mike said. "Who is this guy?"

Alice hesitated. Right, they would want to know this, wouldn't they? She didn't know what to tell them, since nothing she came up with sounded plausible. While Adrianna had been able to accept it, she didn't think anyone else ever would. It was a brother they didn't remember. Nothing about that made sense. But she needed to come up with something. "I…"

A harsh knock rang out from the door. Mike turned back to the computer, his fingers moving across the keyboard to hide windows and show perfectly innocent ones. "Room check!" a voice said on the other side of the door.

Mark turned, but Alice was already gone, turning and appearing again in the bathroom with her back pressed to the wall and crouching down where the mirror would not reflect her into the dorm room. She, however, could see a sliver of what was happening out there as someone walked in. It was a man of barely more than thirty opening the door.

"Everything okay in here?" he asked, looking around the room and taking the long way around to peer at the piles before walking in to the computer. "You guys are being awfully quiet for a Friday night. And awfully still here before ten. What are you up to?"

"Homework," they both said at once. She saw the man standing there for a moment longer, the pair of them looking at him and waiting for him to go away. The minute stretched on and on in a stalemate and no one moved. Alice didn't even breathe, hoping that she didn't get caught. She knew the rules as much as anyone else. You weren't supposed to have girls in the boys dorms or boys in the girls unless they were family. Even then, while you were in the middle school dorms, the door needed to stay open. Otherwise, you needed to be in the common areas.

There was a clunk behind her and she jumped, clapping her hands over her mouth to keep her from letting out any sound to let them know she was there. In the reflection, it seemed that the man had heard it, but more importantly was what caused the clunk.

Matt had dropped down from a spot on the ceiling, landing in the tub. He stopped upon seeing Alice there, then saw the mirror and figured out what was going on. Before the man got the chance to get to the washroom, Matt walked over Alice and out the door. "Hey."

The man looked between the three of them and left, Alice letting out a deep breath that she'd been holding in relief. She was glad to be able to stand up again, and did her best to straighten herself out before she went back out to join them.

"Have we started interrogating her yet?" Matt asked. "Because I want to know how she found our mystery brother."

"She hasn't said yet," Mark said, now all of their eyes were on her. "She hasn't really said much of anything yet."

"Oh good, I got here in time for the fun part," Matt said, cracking his knuckles and twisting his head from one side to the other, a pop sound coming from his neck.

"Hey," Mike said, both him and Mark putting a hand on either shoulder and holding him back. "We go easy on her. One girl alone in a room with three guys and she so much as squeaks too loud and you know what happens to us."

"We aren't going to do anything to her," Matt said, relaxing, but still grinning. "She's just going to tell us everything she knows, right Alice?"

"Uh," Alice started, and she let it hang in the air like a sour note. She really didn't have an answer for them yet and she desperately needed a distraction. Time to think. She would give anything for a chance for her to get the hell out of there right now.

"Can I get a picture of Evan?" she asked, desperately hoping that was enough.

"How do you know this guy?" Mark asked. "Who is he? Why do I think I'm missing a brother?"

Alice hesitated, looking nervously around for some way out and stepping back towards the window. The distance didn't do much good, since there really was nowhere to run without disappearing. They really didn't need to see that. They'd think she was crazy if they saw her do anything out of the ordinary.

"Come on Alice," Mike said. "You can tell us *something*, at least. Is he our long lost brother that none of us know about?"

"Not *long* lost," Alice muttered.

"What?"

"Have you tried looking up Sarah Fitterman?" she asked as a desperate diversion.

"You're changing the subject."

"Why do you think they don't have a file on him?"

"Alice!" Mark snapped at her. "If you didn't want to say anything about it, then you shouldn't have brought it up. Who—"

A scream pierced through the air.

CHAPTER 15

The Source of the Screams

ALICE MANAGED TO cover her ears. It was deafening even though she could tell they were far away from it. She knew what it was and it came just in time, though she did not want it to come at all. The Jabberwocky was back.

She let herself fall to her knees and closed her eyes, trying desperately to block out the thoughts in her mind. The hearts were everywhere around her, beating and beating and beating and not stopping. She needed to run away — to get away from them.

The Queen of Hearts was there too. The blood from the hearts gave birth to her, still on fire with it raging on around her as she melted in the flames. Her skin bubbled and came off in drops, her eyes barely resting in those deep sockets and threatening to drop right out at any sudden movement. She was getting closer, she wanted to touch Alice with her finger that was missing half of the skin and muscle, the bone poking out from the end.

The boys were all dealing with the fear in their own ways of looking like they were going to run or curling up themselves. As she came back to herself, she could see that they were still stuck in their heads as their fear lingered after the echoes of the screams lessened.

She wanted to curl up there and cry as the scream tapered off, but there was work to be done. She needed to find the Jabberwocky and figure out how it got out. She still knew the words to make it quiet again and how to get it to come to her, but she couldn't do that here.

With the brothers too busy in their own heads to notice her, she stepped back towards the window and appeared down on the lawn where she thought the scream came from. Something ran off in the distance, following another scream. Two. There were two Jabberwockys. Screaming at one another, sending the worst images possible directly to the forefront of her mind.

She fought back the fear and chased after it. It was smaller than the Jabberwocky was, but maybe it also knew how to change size. Things in Wonderland did like to do that when they found the right food and she remembered that she found that one in the library. Or maybe this one was just a baby.

She hoped there wasn't a whole nest of them somewhere for her to deal with.

It kept turning sharply on the lawn, making it difficult for Alice to follow until they got into the forest. In here, Alice hated it even more, the dark creature moving between the trees and being tremendously difficult to follow along behind.

Luckily, or unluckily, there was something up ahead that was screaming in a way that sounded like they were getting murdered less violently than the other screams. The fear in her heart was only slowing her feet down rather than stopping her all together.

She went ahead to where the less violent screaming was, certain that this was the worst idea she'd ever had. The trees gave way to an empty area that looked vacant. She stepped in before slowly approaching where the actual screams were coming from.

She walked as softly as she could manage through the brush, having to climb over a fallen branch and through foliage before she reached something she was not expecting. There were no Jabberwockys here. Not even one. There wasn't even anything that looked like they had any sort of teeth at all.

Standing all in a row, nestled next to one another in a long gap between a few large trees and the rocks they were trying to grow into, were strange looking creatures that could possibly be birds. She squinted at them as her eyes adjusted to the darkness. They were furry birds, with large beaks and eyes that looked like they jiggled whenever they moved. Their necks were bare of feathers but, as she could see from the one joining them, they did have very round little bodies and furry feathers that came up almost as a collar. They blended into the colours of the forest around them and Alice was sure that they would have no trouble hiding here if that was what they wanted to do.

They cooed softly at one another, though cooing was the wrong word. Every coo sounded like a nightmare that was playing in someone else's mind that Alice could hear. They were content and didn't even notice Alice as she got closer and closer to them.

Now that she thought about it, the Jabberwocky's cry in Wonderland did not sound like all of her worst fears come to life. Maybe it was just these birds causing the trouble, but Alice didn't know what to do with that information.

If these birds, whatever they were, were the ghost, then they were the things that made everyone disappear? Or were they just there whenever the Jabberwocky took someone? But they didn't seem like they could do anything threatening, unlike the Jabberwocky, who had the claws to remove hearts and the teeth to back them up. These birds were puffs stacked on top of one another and seemed pretty harmless except for their call.

They must have been from Wonderland as well, but how did they get here?

A horrible thought occurred to Alice that made her stomach sink. Did they come out of the book with the Jabberwocky? She might have let out more than just one dragon creature in that night. They might have escaped the book and were just looking for solace in the forest. And the screams all year, they were just the birds trying to find one another.

And now they were sitting here, all in a row and looking content with themselves. The bit on the top of their heads bobbled whenever they tilted their heads, which they did often as they looked around at everything, never seeming to take anything in at all when they did so. Their expressions were so blank and they seemed so unaware of anything that happened around them. She wondered how no one had found them. Sure, she found them because she was looking and they were pretty deep in the forest, but surely they would have been found by now. Someone should have stumbled onto them.

Or maybe they did and disappeared before they could say anything. They were buried in the dark crevice and they would probably only be found either by people who were looking, or by people who literally fell into this nest. She wondered if there were people they kept hidden away beneath them.

Alice needed to get rid of them. She would need to in order to keep anyone else from falling victim to those screams again. To keep herself from falling victim to those screams again.

One of the creatures got its head tassel stuck on a loose bit of bark and struggled to pull itself free. Though even their soft cooing terrified her, Alice couldn't think of these goofy creatures as dangerous. She reached down into the crevice and attempted to untangle it.

Every eye in the crevice bobbled and turned to her at once. In unison, their mouths opened and let out a scream. If Alice were able to think straight, she would have thought the school could hear them screaming so loud. Instead, her mind reeled and spiralled into every dark corner that she had ever been in. The hearts beat in the background as every horrible thing that ever had happened or might have happened to her went through her mind.

She passed out, her throat raw from her own screaming.

CHAPTER 16

Adrianna and the Birds

ALICE WOKE UP screaming. It took her a moment before she realized that she was not surrounded by hearts or on fire or being electrocuted and no one was slowly cutting off her fingers every time they thought she was telling a lie. She wasn't being pulled and stretched or changed into all sorts of shapes she didn't want to be in. She was back in her dormitory, in her bed, and safe. Adrianna was at her side, trying to calm her down.

"It's okay," she said. "It's all right. You're safe now. It's okay."

Alice managed to take a few calming breaths and look around, taking in the lack of the walls beating and closing in on her. She was safe. She was all right. Everything was fine. She was in her bed, still wearing her dirty shoes and clothes. There was light streaming in through the window.

"I'm okay," she said finally. "Everything's okay."

"What happened?" Adrianna asked, sitting next to her and staying close. Alice felt a mix of unease and gratefulness about that. While the company was good, she needed the time to try and forget everything that had happened. All those images, she knew that they were going to follow her and she wanted to just forget them and deal with them later when she was alone. From Adrianna's worried look, she knew that wasn't an option right now.

"I found the ghost," Alice said, smiling half-heartedly. "It turns out it isn't the Jabberwocky that was doing all that screaming. How did I get back here?"

"Mark, Mike, and Matt came in with you after curfew last night," she said. "He said they were all looking for you after you disappeared out of their room. They seemed kind of worried and kind of annoyed."

"Yeah," Alice said, looking nervous. "I almost told them about Evan."

"Evan..." Adrianna's brow knit in concentration and Alice's shoulders dropped. She needed to tell Adrianna who Evan was again. Before she had the chance, Adrianna perked up. "They were looking up Evan. It's a guy that looks like our brother but no one knows who he is. But then you said that he's actually our brother, but the Jabberwocky stole his heart, right? And that made us all forget about him. Right?"

Alice could have hugged her, she was so happy. After last night, Adrianna remembering even that much about Evan was the best news she could have hoped for. Anything to make the horrors of last night fade away faster.

And they were fading away. They left her faster with every waking moment, replaced instead with determination to finish this mess. Evan and his heart. Sarah and her heart. Once those were found, she was done with Wonderland and could go back to normal.

"What day is it?" Alice asked. She felt like she'd asked this a hundred times before.

"Saturday," Adrianna said. "You weren't even gone a whole day this time!"

"Okay." Alice thought about the birds in the forest and Evan. She wasn't going to be able to find Evan if she kept running into those birds over and over again while she was out there. She got to her feet and went to her desk. "I need to try and figure out what to do with the birds."

"Birds?"

"It's the ghost."

"The ghost is birds?"

"It's a whole bunch of birds," Alice said, bringing out the book and her Post-it notes again. "And I need to figure out a new way to make the birds be quiet when we get to them. I don't think we're going to have much fun dealing with them otherwise. I'm surprised that your brothers didn't see them when they found me. I was right next to them."

"They didn't really say anything about that," Adrianna said. "They just said that they were going to get answers out of you one of these days. You've got them really curious, Alice. Maybe you should tell them about Wonderland so they know too."

Alice shook her head. "You and Lori are the only ones I will ever tell about Wonderland. Everyone else I tell just thinks I'm crazy. But I am really happy you believe me," Alice added, smiling and looking back at her. "I really needed someone to believe me."

Adrianna smiled and sat back, watching as Alice went through the book, finding the entry she needed fairly quickly. She'd flipped past it several times before. There was an obvious blank spot on the page for a picture. The entry was for Jubjub birds.

Alice had heard that before. Someone had said it to her recently. She found herself absently rubbing her arm, remembering when Cat sank his claws deep into her disobedient flesh. That was it. The Cheshire Cat said he would leave the Jabberwocky to hunt the Jubjub birds in the forest where he would be content and he wouldn't have to do a damn thing to control it. He knew about the Jubjub birds.

"He knew," Alice said. "He knew that something came out of the book with the Jabberwocky."

"What?" Adrianna asked. "Who knew?"

"Cat. Cat knew that the Jubjub birds were out of the book too. He knows something."

"What are you going to do about it?" Adrianna asked.

Alice thought about it and her mind went places she really didn't want it to go. Cat might have tried to sell her to the Queen of Hearts in exchange for being able to cross the mirror, and she definitely didn't want to see him again, but he knew more about what else got out of the book than she did. At this point, she needed all the information she could get on that, even if it meant going back to talk to him again.

"Maybe figure out how to get rid of the birds first," Alice said. If she could delay seeing Cat again, she would. "Maybe there's a way to put them back into the book. Or I could lure them away somehow and leave them in the forest somewhere."

"I'm helping this time," Adrianna said. "The Jabberwocky liked me. Maybe the birds will too."

Alice didn't really want to argue that logic. As much as she didn't want to get anyone else involved, she could not handle hearing the birds on her own. The things they brought up in her were not things she ever wanted to relive again if she could help it and Adrianna *had* been able to handle the Jabberwocky better than she had. Maybe she could just wear her headphones to block out the sound.

They didn't go back to finding the birds right away. Alice needed to figure out how to change the phrase around so that she could silence birds, and Adrianna had to teach her to say the words. She kept referencing the page on the Jubjub birds, trying to make sure that she had the right description.

The Jubjub birds, which were what Cat said they likely were, were mostly harmless. Even without the picture, Alice was still able to figure out that this was the right page. It talked about how their call was like a scream that brought a person down into the darkest depths of their mind. It was their only form of self defense and thankfully worked very well, because they didn't have any other way of protecting themselves. They liked small, narrow crevices and dark places. When they got lost, they let out a screech, to find one another, though often they would forget that they were lost at all and sometimes stood in a single spot for months at a time, trying to remember what they were trying to do.

Alice remembered their eyes and the big dumb looks they gave her. She could believe that. They were not the brightest and she wasn't about to believe that they were the ones taking hearts. The book said that a flock would actually eat a tree once every few months as a means of sustenance, then not eat at all until they found another one. They were known to nest in the cracks caused from the fallen tree they feasted on and would scatter all other animals out of the area with their coos, which were not as harsh as their calls.

Alice could silence them, but she wasn't sure if she could send them back to Wonderland. If they didn't go willingly back, then she would need to find a mirror to lead them through. After the last time, she wanted to avoid setting foot back in Wonderland and avoid seeing either Cat or the Jabberwocky again.

The Jabberwocky seemed terrified the entire time he was there, but it was from Wonderland. He should have been happy to go back and not be trapped in a book this time. It might be because he could smell the Queen of Hearts and her influence changing things. Even Alice could feel it when she was there, like a dark cloud devouring the land.

Weird that the Jabberwocky couldn't talk, though. She wondered if the Jubjub birds could do anything but let out terrifying screams that made Alice linger on thoughts of death and torture.

"I don't know if this is going to be right," Alice said finally, slamming the book closed. "And I don't know how to make them go into Wonderland this time. I don't know what to do."

"Maybe we should just go see them," Adrianna suggested, looking a little too excited to see the nightmare-inducing birds. "We need to make sure they didn't go anywhere, right?"

Alice could think of nothing else she could do at this point. The weather was brighter now, so they could fairly easily get through the woods and it wouldn't even be unusual. There were science classes sent into the woods to collect samples as homework, so they would blend in. Well, until they went deeper into the woods.

"I hope they haven't gone too far," Alice said, getting up and putting on a pair of shoes. Adrianna was right behind her, grabbing a sweater just in case and tying it around her waist before they went out into the rest of the building.

They got as far as the stairs before Alice saw trouble. One of Adrianna's brothers was walking past and looked up. Alice ducked back behind Adrianna and stepped out into the sunshine just outside the dormitory doors. She pressed her back against the door, now being propped open to let in the breeze, and waited for Adrianna to catch up.

"Hold up," she heard just before Adrianna got to the door.

"Hey Mike," she said. Alice could hear the hesitation. She probably just noticed that Alice wasn't behind her anymore.

"Where is she?"

"What?"

"I saw Alice with you just a minute ago," Mike said. "Where is she?"

"She's not here."

"Look, is something up with her?" Mike asked, sounding genuinely concerned. "What's her deal?"

"She's just really busy."

"Busy doesn't leave you unconscious in a forest, Addie. If she's getting involved with anything—"

"She's fine. She knows what she's doing."

"So there *is* something going on."

"She's just trying to find Evan. Once she does, she's done."

"These aren't the kind of secrets you keep, Addie."

"You worry too much."

Adrianna came through the door a few moments later. Alice waited for her to walk a few steps out of sight of the door before she ran to catch up. She was grateful to Adrianna for not saying anything, but worried about how easy that conversation had gone. How often had Adrianna had to defend Alice to her brothers already?

"Sorry," Alice said as she fell in step next to Adrianna.

"Mike was looking for you," she said. "I think they're worried about you."

Alice didn't say anything more, instead walking quietly into the woods with Adrianna. They saw other people out there, some in the midst of a big game of capture the flag while others were collecting samples or taking a run along the paths. Alice wondered how many people took their chance to go to the glass cave where the Jabberwocky had been hiding. It was a lot nicer now with him gone.

"Do you know what you're going to do?" Adrianna asked once they seemed to be far enough away. Alice led the way, trying to remember the zig zags that the bird took through the forest. It wasn't as easy a path to find as following behind the Jabberwocky, but there was one easy way to tell. The number of animals lessening.

"Not yet," Alice said. "I mean, maybe I can convince them to go back to Wonderland, but if I have to lure them through like the Jabberwocky, I don't know how I'd get back. And I don't know how I'd get a mirror all the way out here."

"So you aren't going to talk to Cat?"

Alice shook her head. "Not if I don't have to," she said. "He tried to sell me to the Queen of Hearts. I don't really want to talk to him ever again."

"But he knows more about what they are and what the Jabberwocky is, right?"

"And he probably knows if anything else came out of the book that night," Alice agreed. "I don't know. He might know how to get rid of the Jubjub birds, but I don't think so. He wanted to just leave everything here and let the Jabberwocky eat the birds and I guess keep taking people's hearts. I still haven't been able to find those hearts."

"It's all right," Adrianna said. "You'll find them. But it's not so bad since we can't really remember. And I don't think Evan would be very happy to find out he missed so many exams when he gets back."

Alice smiled sadly and kept moving forward. She didn't know how she'd take learning that she had a sister that she couldn't remember. It wouldn't be as well as Adrianna did. She had too much faith in Alice. It was like she knew some-how Alice would get him back, but Alice wasn't only trying to get him back. There was Sarah too, who wasn't around long enough to be found in clippings or to have appeared in some-one else's student files. At least, not that she knew of.

Alice brought them to a halt as she saw the rocks and the tree where the Jubjub birds hid the last time. In the air, there were the faint coos that sounded like little screams of people who weren't expecting a band aid to be ripped off so suddenly. Adrianna heard them too, but she didn't see them or know where they were until Alice turned to face them.

With one hand out, Alice said, "*Ábedecian swég angrisla wudufugol sugian,*" moving her hand and thinking only of the quiet she wanted them to be. The coos and cries stopped instantly, Alice letting out a breath of relief that she wouldn't have to worry about their screams any longer.

She turned to wave Adrianna over, though Adrianna hesi-tated before coming any closer. Alice looked back and found a head was sticking up out of the crevice between the rocks and the tree, the tassel on it bobbing behind it and the large beak swinging around to face her. Even both wild eyes faced her. Then another one came up. And then more.

Oh boy. She made them mad.

Their mouths opened, but nothing came out. Where the Jabberwocky barely seemed to notice, these birds just kept trying and failing to let out any sound, tilting their head from one side to another before trying again. They started to do so in unison in a very strange show that Alice wasn't sure she wanted to stick around for.

Though Alice started to back up, Adrianna moved forward, curious about the creatures that were hiding down there. They looked harmless and Adrianna probably didn't think they could do anything to hurt her.

"Adrianna," Alice said warningly. "I don't think they're very happy."

"They just look a little confused," Adrianna said. "Probably wondering where their voices went. I'd be confused too."

She kept getting closer. The birds, one by one, turned to look at her instead of Alice and Alice was ready to get her out of there. They would have to run, Alice remembered, as she didn't come with her when she tried to step away.

A line of birds leaned backwards and their legs came up, stepping out of the crevice and fluttering closer to Adrianna. Adrianna didn't move away, laughing instead as they bobbed towards her and surrounded her in a small flock. The next line did the same, all of them looking up at her and chirping silently as she tried to give them all the attention they seemed to want.

"Come on now," she said to the flock around her. "Wait your turn. It's okay. I'll say hi to all of you."

Alice was sure that they weren't that nice to her when she saw them before. She approached them slowly, seeing Adrianna doing so well with them. Maybe she caught them at a bad time before. She had just chased them through the woods. She wanted to help, but at night it might not have looked that way.

When Alice got close, three of the birds in the back all turned their heads as one to face her, followed by turning the rest of their bodies. Alice slowed down and stopped, looking down at all of them. She bent down a little to get a better look. All three reached out with their beaks and started trying to snap at her.

"Hey!" Alice yelped, jumping back from them. Once she was a few paces away, they turned back to Adrianna, who looked like she was having no problems at all with her new found fame among the Jubjub birds.

"They don't like you very much," Adrianna said.

"Apparently only cats like me," Alice said, taking a seat on a rock outside of their reach and not stopping Adrianna from enjoying the flock. As much as the birds didn't like Alice and made her nervous with their screeches, Adrianna looked comfortable around them. She talked to them and cooed at them. When she sang, they pretended that they could sing along. Alice hoped she would never actually hear them sing.

They weren't so bad when they were quiet. So long as Alice wasn't going close to them, they were affectionate, even if they looked pretty silly. Maybe if they just learned to not scream like that, then she could leave them there, but she hadn't seen anything in the book that would do that. There wasn't even anything to make them permanently quiet.

She'd let them out and they couldn't stay. They didn't belong here. They belonged in Wonderland, or at least back in the book, but she didn't know how to do either. Here, she'd learned what happened when there was a creature with no natural predators. Cat was right on that front at least. Without the Jabberwocky around to keep their population low, they would breed, and when they did that they would continue to scream in all the crevices they could find.

"I have to go back," Alice said finally, defeated. Adrianna perked up from the Jubjub birds to listen with a noise to let Alice know she was definitely paying attention. "I'm going to have to go back and talk to the Cheshire Cat."

When she said it, she knew she had to do it. On top of these birds, he might know where the Jabberwocky had hidden away the hearts. And he could tell her if there was any-thing else that escaped from the book besides just these birds and the Jabberwocky. She worried that there was something else dangerous that might have gotten out.

Her mind flashed back to the four white eyes. She shud-dered.

"Are you sure?" Arianna asked.

Alice nodded. "He knows. I don't know how I'm going to get back yet, though. I might have to…"

"To what?"

Alice looked off into the woods. Something else was moving back there in the distance. It walked slowly and mechanically, whatever it was. It was too small to be a bear, too thin to be one too, but there was definitely something back there. It didn't seem to have noticed them, but that wasn't the point. It didn't look like any animal Alice had ever seen before and there shouldn't be any other students this far out in the woods.

"What is that?" Adrianna asked, standing and looking out in that direction.

"Can you find your way back on your own?" Alice asked.

"Alice, I don't think it's a good idea," she said. "You don't know what that is. It's not even coming after us. Maybe it's just someone who got lost."

"I hope so," Alice said, taking a few steps forward. She

was behind a tree several feet away a moment later, peering out around it to get a better look.

CHAPTER 17

The Bandersnatch's Proposal

THERE WAS NOTHING there, but another figure appeared a little farther away. Given Alice's luck, the first one probably ran off because it didn't like her, so she went to the next one. That one vanished when she got too close. They weren't running away; they just weren't there anymore. She kept trying, but they kept moving.

Growing annoyed, Alice tried walking instead of trying to sneak up on them. The figure didn't vanish when she did that, still moving away at exactly the same slow rate as before. She was able to get closer to it now, following behind at a fair pace so that she could keep her distance in case she needed to run.

As it came clearer into view, she knew that she'd made a mistake. It wasn't a spindly creature at all, but a person. A person wearing a blue blazer and a black and white checkered skirt. She had long brown hair tied up in a ponytail and she was almost transparent, though getting sharper and denser in focus with every step she went. She went from being a blur in the distance to a student that Alice had never seen before.

This was not what the Jabberwocky's victims were like in Wonderland at all. They didn't fade away and get stronger depending on where they were in Wonderland. They were just as lifeless, sure, but there was no aspect of fading away. Alice wondered if this girl was one of the people the Jabberwocky took or if she was something else entirely.

Maybe the Jabberwocky's victims got stronger when they got closer to their hearts, wherever they were hidden. If that were the case, then she just had to follow them back and hopefully figure out how to put the hearts back once she found them. This was good. She could finally get Evan and Sarah back. Maybe whoever else was taken by the Jabberwocky would be around here, too.

She moved faster to keep up. Despite how bright it was a moment ago, dense fog rolled in and Alice was starting to think this might be a bad idea. She was so close, though, and she wasn't willing to turn back now. She was sure they passed a barrier this far out and that this was off campus, but she was so close.

The fog became too dense and Alice made a sprint forward to grab the girl. The girl passed right through Alice's fingers. Alice looked at her hand for a moment, confused, and then searched the fog again for the girl. The fog was so dense that she couldn't even tell where she had come from a moment before, much less where she went. She tried taking a few steps to put herself outside the fog, but didn't get anywhere.

The fog broke all of a sudden and she stepped into something quite unlike the forest. Night was above her, the stars twinkling even though it was barely afternoon. Around her, there were no trees but something of a room with walls made out of curtains of fog. There were things stacked in a pile along one side, all things that might have been brought out of a dorm room. Suitcases with clothes, dressing mirrors, computers, and books, all piled along one side and out of the way of everything else.

Throughout the space, there were silver statues and empty pedestals. She saw the girl climb up onto one, standing there for a moment perfectly still before she turned to silver. Alice hesitated, and then went over to walk through them, finding people she didn't know among their number. There were a couple students and someone who looked like a teacher. There was huge man in a uniform that looked like it was meant for extermination. She wondered if he was the one sent to take care of the bear.

Evan was there a little farther down the line. Alice ran to

see him, looking up to find him just standing on the pedestal and staring forward at nothing at all. He looked fine except for being silver, with none of the hole in his chest that Alice was so worried about. He was so shiny that Alice could see herself in him.

Sarah was even there. A dozen or so figures just stood there, frozen in silver and not prey to the Jabberwocky at all. There were still so many empty pedestals around that Alice had to wonder if maybe there were more people who were still out wandering the woods.

"Evan?" she asked, since she was closest to him. She tapped him, trying to see if the metal was solid or just a coat. He sounded solid and she tried to stay calm. "Evan, can you hear me?"

"None of them can hear you, child."

Alice snapped up and looked around. She couldn't see anything that spoke to her. Nothing around her moved, nothing made a sound but her. There wasn't even another smell in the air to let her know that she wasn't alone.

"Quite a wonderful collection, don't you agree? They all came to me, you know. Not how I like to do things, but good for the beginnings of a collection."

Alice tried to take a few steps and get out of there, thinking about the dorms. When she didn't leave, she tried to get to the Jubjub birds, then just out to the forest, and found that she was still here. It wasn't working. She tried again, sliding behind one of the people and going nowhere else.

"That's not going to work in here, child."

Alice turned to find herself face to face with four white eyes set in a darkness that was like solid shadow. She jumped back to find it was a creature Alice couldn't quite place. It was sleek as a wolf and hunched over to stick its face right over her shoulder. It was as big as a bear, but it didn't look like one of those either. The way it held itself was regal and terrifying. It had no teeth or claws, but Alice didn't doubt that it could snuff her out in an instant if it wanted to.

She realized after a moment of holding her breath that it was shifting forms as she watched it. That's why she couldn't tell what it looked like beyond those four eyes and that feeling that it was tremendously powerful. She didn't remember reading anything about the Jabberwocky being able to do this in the book. She wasn't sure that this was a Jabberwocky at all.

"I am not anything so mundane as a Jabberwocky, child," he said. He grew until he was as tall as the trees and even more massive. He shrunk back down again to something Alice didn't have to strain her neck to look at, but she was still wide-eyed and too scared to move. She couldn't even get out of there and the creature seemed interested in her. Even without pupils, she could tell he was looking at her with all four eyes.

"You smell of Wonderland, child." He was amused. His voice sounded like the darkness, of that fear in the back of her mind she had when she was little, of the things she thought lurked in the dark before she learned that there was plenty in the light to be scared of. "We have met before."

"Who are you?" Alice managed to finally get out. Her back was pressed against the bear catcher's legs. "What is this place?"

The creature looked amused. "Ah, now there's a voice I recognize. You were the one who did me the kindness of releasing me." He bowed, a laugh coming out of him that made Alice's skin crawl. "I am the Bandersnatch. It is good to finally be free of that book. And of that Queen."

He said the last word as a curse, looking away from Alice and his body writhing in anger. A long ceramic claw came out of one hand, twitching in threat. Alice backed up another step, but the Bandersnatch didn't care, heading around to one end of the room where there was a large cushion covered in crushed velvet to take a seat.

"Come child," he said, waving a claw at her. Alice appeared in front of him and a seat appeared behind her legs, knocking her into sitting on it. "Wonderland's champion shall come to no harm this day. As my thanks for the release. Enjoy this privilege while you may."

"Thank you," Alice said, though she wasn't quite sure

why. He was just agreeing not to hurt her. She wasn't sure why she should be thanking anyone for simply not hurting her, but she knew well enough not to make him mad. The Bandersnatch was clearly nothing to trifle with.

"Such good manners," the Bandersnatch said. He was smiling and Alice could make out very sharp teeth as white as porcelain and sharper than anything Alice had ever seen. "I expect far worse than that of Wonderland. I must admit, my time in Wonderland was quite terrible. I see you have not quite enjoyed your visits either. Ah, but you do not want to talk of that place."

Alice wasn't sure how he knew what she was thinking, but his eyes went back to the people he had. His collection, he called them. "I assure you they are all perfectly safe. They were all fairly traded or wandered in on their own wishing to do me harm, so I have decided to keep them. So many more have been coming in since the Jabberwocky left, though. Not quite the way I like to do business, but who am I to turn away food that walks onto my plate?"

"Food?" Alice asked, finding her voice as small as she felt. "You're going to eat them?"

"Nothing quite so vulgar as you are thinking, child. Do you have a name?"

"Alice Liddell," she said, though she didn't really want to give it to him. She didn't know what came over her.

"Nothing so vulgar as eating their flesh, Alice Liddell." He left his throne and went over to the bear catcher. "No, I just eat a few years off the top at a time. This one has plenty of years to go through."

She watched as he passed over the statue of a man. He melted from the silver as he was being absorbed into the Bandersnatch's body and a look of terror covered his face. No screams escaped, though Alice knew he tried. The Bandersnatch passed over him and peeled himself off, leaving him on the pedestal. She watched as it looked like an outer shell peeled off of the man and the Bandersnatch slurped it back up. The man stared out with a horrified look in his eyes as he reformed in silver, looking five years younger.

"That will satisfy me for a while," the Bandersnatch said, leaving nothing of the shell of the man behind. He melted into the air and reformed back on his throne, though Alice was still staring at the man he had just eaten.

"It's only their years, Alice Liddell," he said. "No need to look so horrified. They won't even remember them."

"What did you do to them?" she asked, tearing her eyes away from the bear catcher. She was in a lot of trouble, but she forced herself to stay calm. "Will they ever leave here?"

"They may leave when someone who still remembers them does me a favour," the Jabberwocky said. "Or if they should win a bet. That is how I do business. I also much prefer it if people are brought to me in exchange for favours. This having them walk into my realm nonsense is hardly any fun at all."

"You want people to give you other people?"

"In exchange for a favour, yes," he said as if explaining it to a small child. Alice felt like a very small child right now. "I am nothing if not fair. A few of these were gifts in exchange for another's freedom. They did not understand the chance they had in their hands, I'm afraid, but there are those who would sacrifice the people they love to get what they want, Alice Liddell. I enjoy such ambition. If anyone were willing to do a thing like that, why wouldn't I oblige them? I may be a powerful creature, but it amuses me so to see what others will do to try to gain even the smallest fraction of my power."

Alice didn't doubt for an instant that he was the most powerful creature she'd ever met. She could imagine him being able to do whatever he wanted. She knew that she feared him.

"Ah, but you wanted to know about the other part," the Bandersnatch said, amused. "You see, when I take someone, I make sure they are taken. When you enter my realm, you cease to exist outside of here. It means I gain a bit of a collection —" he waved at the collection of things piled up on the side of the room he'd created out of fog "— but I do quite like to see how many things I can gather. Sometimes all a person needs is something in the pile of things I collect from my meals. It makes the exchange much easier than granting them whatever they are looking for. Such mundane things. Power. Wealth. Love. Very dull, you see."

Alice looked around, hardly able to understand what was going on. She saw Sarah turn back to flesh and come down from her pedestal, walking out into the fog barrier.

"That one needs some more aging," the Bandersnatch said by way of explanation. "Many of them do. So I permit them to wander now and then."

"How do I get them back?" Alice asked, turning back to the Bandersnatch. "What do I have to do to make you let them go?"

Though he had no mouth at the moment, she knew there was a smile in that inky blackness. "You want to do a favour for the one you remember?" he asked, sounding quite amused. "I suppose I can do you that kindness for releasing me."

"Can't I take one for letting you free?" Alice asked.

The Bandersnatch was not amused. "I am not adding you to my garden," he said. "That is reward enough for that kindness. But you may do me a different favour. I am tired of having people wandering in and presenting themselves as food. It hardly seems fair. Find a way to keep out the unworthy and I'll return one of them to you."

"What if I want to get all of them out?" Alice asked. "What would I have to do to get all of them out?"

The suggestion did not amuse him. "You don't," he said. "You may only barter for those you remember. None of the others are available to you."

"But I can't just leave them here," Alice said, looking back at them and her mind racing. "I don't know who they are, but that doesn't mean that you can just have them. You can't keep them here!"

The Bandersnatch grew large in front of her and Alice stumbled back out of her chair. "You are in my realm," he said, his voice loud and clearly displeased as he advanced on Alice. She kept backing up further and further until she bumped against the pedestal that Evan stood on. "In here, you do not get to decide what I can and cannot do, child."

"I'm sorry," Alice managed to stammer out. She needed to get out of here, but she couldn't fade away like she usually did. Not in here. She would go anywhere right now, even Wonderland, if it meant getting away. "I didn't mean to offend you."

"Wonderland. You even smell of Wonderland. I should have known that you would have the manners of Wonderland as well. Do you understand who I am, Alice Liddell?"

Alice pressed herself into the pedestal as hard as she could and fell backwards into the light.

CHAPTER 18

Painted Mirrors

ALICE BOUNCED OFF the large mushroom and landed on a smaller patch of mushrooms. With the wind knocked out of her, she looked up at the sky to find no clouds and a bright blue day that was a lot warmer than where she came from.

Underneath her, something squirmed and vanished from under her back, the purple cat appearing on her chest and looking very displeased. "Quite rude of you to drop in like that."

Alice took in a breath and could not stop coughing. She rolled to her side as her lungs protested her attempts to refill them. They were on fire and her mind was reeling. She knew where the missing people were and they were thankfully much fewer in number than she thought. A dozen people, and less than ten of them were students. Most were even from the high school, so she didn't feel bad about not knowing they were missing.

The Jabberwocky, though, was preferable to the Bandersnatch. While the Jabberwocky was a dragon that looked like it was willing to bite her in two, the Bandersnatch did something else entirely. Watching it eat was something that unsettled her. Taking years off the top was nothing she understood and she didn't know what it was she saw him do in the least. Didn't old people like becoming younger? She didn't understand what he was doing.

And he had those claws. He was the claw that came out of the book that stole the hearts.

She took a deep breath to settle herself before sitting up. She was immediately pushed back down by the large cat, his claws back in her face and the Cheshire Cat's grin turning quite sinister. "Hello Alice," he said. "Very nice of you to drop in without a word of apology."

Alice wasn't scared of this anymore. Not after everything else that she'd been through in the last couple days. Something about sharp objects in her face was really bland at this point. Maybe if he had a knife instead of his cat claws, then she might be scared. But not those claws.

"Hello Cat," Alice said. "I have to admit, as much as I never wanted to see you again I'm really glad to see you. I was going to come looking for you soon."

Cat withdrew his claws and looked at her curiously. He tilted his head and peered closer, putting his face right up into

Alice's, but she didn't move. Not that she could with the Cat standing on top of her. "Such a delightful change that you have finally embraced your madness."

"Don't get too excited," Alice said, sitting up and pushing him off of her. He stepped off and stayed at her side as she stepped off the mushroom patch. "It's just been a really bad day."

"Perhaps the badness is to make you understand how poorly you acted when you were here last," Cat suggested. He did not sound pleased. "You were quite rude. Attacking a queen is quite disrespectful, as is rejecting a very generous offer. And, let us not forget, there's what you did to my fur."

Cat bristled and shook out his fur as if to illustrate just how much she had ruined it. "Did your mother never teach you to not throw your friends?"

Alice laughed. "That would imply that we're friends. And you *tried to sell me to the Queen of Hearts.*"

"And yet you still return for my company."

This was getting her nowhere. She still had to figure out how to get back out of Wonderland from here and she had no idea where she even was yet, much less how to get back to her dorm before the weekend was out. She didn't really have time for Cat and his riddles. Straight-forward as she could be, then. And wandering around until Wonderland gave her some clue as to how to get her out of there.

"You knew about the Jubjub birds," Alice said as she started walking. The Cheshire Cat followed along at her shoulder. "You knew about the Jabberwocky coming out of the book, too. What else came out of the book with them?"

"Why, I presume anything else that you decided to set free," the Cheshire Cat said with a wide, puzzled grin. "You would know better than I, dear. You were the one reading it. I simply watched and waited to see how quickly the madness would set in after you finished."

"It hasn't," Alice said, glaring daggers at him.

"It is not good to hold your anger so close, Alice," he said, clicking his tongue in disappointment. "Anger has a way of spilling over in waves and rivers, much like sadness. And you remember the last time you let your sadness spill over in Wonderland."

Alice pictured the lava of her anger spilling over and sweeping Cat away with everyone else. That would be a nice way to get rid of him, but he was still next to her, smiling and waiting for her to react again. Alice did not oblige.

"Come now, Alice," he said, sounding amused and like he'd figured out what was going on. "Don't tell me you didn't pay attention. Especially after someone went through all the trouble of writing such a thing. Even I know better than to ignore the words that someone so meticulously worked on."

"What else came out of the book with the Jabberwocky?"

she asked. She was kicking herself for not thinking to go back to that first page and look it over again. She couldn't remember what was written on it anymore, but as Cat pondered, she hoped that he could remember.

"Let me see," he said, drifting in front of her and stopping her from going any further, "if I remember correctly, which mind you I always do, there was the Jabberwocky, the Jubjub birds and something called a Bandersnatch. That sounded like nothing that you would want to cross, so I daresay that was the one you had to worry about."

He wasn't wrong. It was unfortunate that he didn't know more than that, but it was probably all you could really gather from the one poem. It wasn't that long and there was mostly stuff on the Jabberwocky in there that she could remember.

"Do you know how to put them back?" It was the last thing she needed to know. After that, she would step out of here and far away to something else that could annoy her but still lead her out. Maybe another mirror had opened up somewhere.

There had to be a way back out of Wonderland.

Cat looked at her in amusement before drifting out of her path and letting her walk again. "You were like a key, Alice. And the poem like a lock. You set them free and you will need to find a way to contain them once more. It is hardly my job to figure out your job." He laughed, a cruel and terrible laugh.

"I may know a great many things that will assist your ability to do that. It will not be free, though. You do not expect a cat to deliver anything for free. I may be able to help, however, in exchange for a favour."

The word *favour* sent a chill up her spine. She didn't like having to do one just to release a single person, one that wasn't even going to release more than one student or other person at a time. It was her fault they were all stuck there because she let the damn thing out. She had to get this all cleaned up.

She took a few steps and was out of there. She knew what Cat wanted, but she was not willing to let him back through. She wanted everything to be back in Wonderland so she could continue her life at Lucena Academy. She could be normal. People might stop thinking she was weird because she was disappearing all the time to deal with Wonderland stuff.

"I take it you had a run in with the Bandersnatch." The Cheshire Cat was next to her again back in the field where the mirror lay broken into a thousand little pieces. No one had cleaned it up yet, but it looked like someone was rolling all the bits together to make little mirror men like it was snow. "He did not seem like the one to cross, if I'm remembering the words right."

Alice was getting very good at ignoring Cat as he floated around her. She just kept walking and a few paces later she was somewhere else. A mirror. She needed a mirror. They couldn't have destroyed every mirror in Wonderland.

"Ah, have you already crossed him, perhaps?" Cat asked. "No matter. I'm sure you can find some way to refrain from being rude long enough for a conversation. Just because you've yet to do so to my knowledge doesn't mean you never will, of course."

"But I suppose you'd smooth things over for me if I would just allow you back across the mirror?"

"Well, if you're being so kind as to offer."

"No," Alice said firmly. "Why would you even want to come back over now that the Bandersnatch is there?"

"Because, Alice, you must keep your friends close and your enemies as far away from you as possible."

"I thought you were supposed to keep them closer."

"Why would I want my enemies close?" Cat looked at her like she'd gone crazy. "If they were close, I would have to talk to them, and that is not what I want. No, I would much rather have them as far as possible and I have made a few enemies in my time in Wonderland. In your world, however, I have none! It seems like a wondrous place to be."

"But the Bandersnatch—"

"Ah, but I have not met the Bandersnatch yet," Cat said. "And, thanks to you, I will know to avoid him." He sounded pleased with himself for that.

Alice let out a noise of irritation and shook her head. She appeared in another part of Wonderland and walked in on two familiar boys arguing and pushing one another. Cat had not followed yet, so Alice decided to talk to these two. She needed a mirror. Someone had to have something that was a reflective surface somewhere. A large random piece of silver. A particularly shiny chrome fridge. Anything.

"No, I am!" one of them said, pushing a little too hard and sending the other boy right into Alice.

Alice caught him, but he shook himself out of Alice's hands and went right back at his brother. "No, me!"

"Hello," Alice said loudly, interrupting their fight and drawing the attention to herself. "Is everything alright?"

"It is not!" Tweedle Dum said. "You have gotten in the middle of a perfectly good argument!"

"It's not an argument!" his brother said. "It's a squabble!"

Alice hated Wonderland sometimes.

"I am terribly sorry for my interruption," Alice said. It was time to play Wonderland's game. "I'm afraid I am looking for something and do not know where I will ever manage to find it. But I suppose you both are far too busy to assist me in something like that."

They both eyed her suspiciously, and then asked at once, "What are you looking for?"

"Why, only a mirror," Alice said.

"Isn't she the one who was going to be a princess?" Twee-dle Dee asked his brother.

"The one who we gave to the Queen of Hearts?" Tweedle Dum asked. They recognized her. Alice didn't know if this was good or not yet, but she could see the Cheshire Cat's eyes nearby, watching from the bushes and trying to decide if he should interrupt.

"She probably needs to see if she's pretty," Tweedle Dee said. "Princesses always need to know if they're pretty."

"No, princesses need to see if they are *attractive*."

"Do you know where I might find one?" Alice asked quickly, hoping to cut through their argument. They both looked at her and seemed to wonder if she was daft.

"You should look in a house," Tweedle Dee said. "That's where people usually keep them."

"There are no mirrors in any houses that I've seen today," Alice said. It was technically the truth, but she hadn't looked inside any houses. She still knew that there were no reflective surfaces left that she could use to get home in Wonderland right now. "And I do so need to see my face soon."

"There are mirrors inside them!" Tweedle Dum insisted. "You just need to look under the paint."

Alice looked at both of them flatly, her dramatics fading into nothing. "Paint?"

The boys nodded. "The Cheshire Cat said that the Queen

was using them to find everyone in Wonderland and get them. He said we needed to cover them so she couldn't see through them and find us anymore, so we went over all of Wonderland and covered all the mirrors in paint so she couldn't find us."

"Paint?!" Alice demanded, her eyes moving from the boys to the purple ones off in the distance. They were not there anymore, but she knew that Cat knew full well that he'd been caught. If she ever saw him again, she was going to kick him clear across Wonderland into a lake somewhere and hope he drowned.

"We went all through Wonderland and got all of them!" They sounded far too proud of themselves.

"You did an excellent job," Alice said through a clenched jaw and forced herself to smile. No wonder she couldn't find anything reflective left. They had probably coated every single thing in fear that the Queen of Hearts would find them.

"I did most of the work," Tweedle Dee said. "He just held the paint."

"Holding the paint *is* most of the work!"

Alice didn't even care about their fighting anymore. She just needed to think of a place that would have had a mirror that she could go to. She hadn't actually been inside too many houses in Wonderland that she could think of. The castle was a definite no. She'd had more than enough of running into the Queen of Hearts to last her for quite a while.

The White Rabbit's house came to mind right as one of the twins slammed into her, having been pushed by his brother. She let out a cry and went flying backwards and found herself falling instead of landing hard on the ground. The one that bumped into her bounced back towards his brother and out of sight.

Alice felt panic about falling for only a moment. She'd done a lot of falling today. At this point, she just went with it. She would head back home, eat something and Adrianna would hear all about all of this.

She knew this hole. The rabbit hole that was the very first thing she'd ever encountered of Wonderland so many years ago. It looked the same as it did before, with things floating there and not telling her that she was rude as she fell up past them. She liked it in here and, if she could manage it, this would be where she came instead of Wonderland next time. She wondered if there was a mirror in here that she could use.

CHAPTER 19

Memory Loss

WHEN HER BACK hit the dirt, the world around her flipped and the wind flew out of her again. The hole got a lot smaller and she had to crawl out, ending up covered in dirt. The day was a lot darker now and Alice really hoped that it wasn't too late.

It was hard to see through the mist and she could feel where the Bandersnatch was, the fog calling to her with promises of power and whatever she could possibly desire. She tried to step away, but moving like that felt like she was moving through mud and she couldn't get very far when she did. She got a couple trees away and decided it wasn't worth it, instead walking on foot until the fog let up, revealing the late afternoon sun in the sky.

At least she wasn't going to be caught for being back too late. She managed to cross the rest of the forest in a few steps.

Adrianna was no longer with the Jubjub birds and the birds all looked like they were back in their little alcove. They still cooed with their little screams, their voices returned to them and none seeking to leave their crevice. That was good, at least.

She went across campus and into the dorms, appearing just inside the door to find Adrianna coming out of the shower. She stopped at the door, looking confused at Alice and pulling her towel tighter around herself.

Alice smiled and waved weakly. "Sorry about that," Alice said, feeling bad that she'd left her alone in the forest. "I promise I'll stop leaving you behind. Did you manage to get back all right?"

Adrianna looked curiously at her. She hadn't moved since Alice started talking to her. There was a long moment of silence. Alice worried that she'd done something to make Adrianna very angry. She didn't look mad, though. She looked more confused than anything.

Finally, she started to speak. "Alice?" she said, her brow furrowing as she tried to think. "I know you, right?"

"I'm your friend," Alice said slowly, confused and worried. "And I live here with you." Alice looked around the room to find that half of her things were missing. Her breath caught in the back of her throat and she had to force herself to breathe again. The Bandersnatch couldn't have made her disappear, could he?

Alice didn't move as Adrianna went to grab some clothes and changed in the bathroom. Around her, her things started to appear again and she took a seat at the door, trying to think. The Bandersnatch said something about this. That everyone who came into his realm was forgotten, but she hadn't been in his realm for a while. She went to Wonderland, but apparently that hadn't reset her existence.

When Adrianna came out, her eyes lit up at the sight of her. "Alice!" she said, fully recognizing her at last. "I don't know what happened. It was like I completely forgot who you were. I remember being in the forest with the Jubjubs, but then I forgot what I was doing there and I came back. And then I was with Heather for a while and Mike was trying to figure out why there was stuff on his computer and... what happened?"

Alice let out a happy breath of relief. "Dinner?" she asked. "I'm starving. I'll tell you everything."

They went to the cafeteria and grabbed their meals, but they were not alone. Heather waved them both over to join them, Robert and Kevin at their table. Alice promised she'd tell Adrianna afterwards and Adrianna led the way, both of them setting their trays down.

"You have got to stop being so weird," Heather told Alice

as they started on their dinner. "Mark spent half an hour just asking me what your deal was."

"My deal?" Alice asked.

"Don't worry. I just told him you were actually a 45 year old male CIA agent rooming with his sister."

"So you're seeing Mark now?" Kevin asked. "Can you even tell them apart?"

"I know which one is Mark. Still can't quite get Mike and Matt. Sorry, Adrianna."

"It's okay," Adrianna told her. "They like it that way."

"I don't know what you did, but the three of them are determined to figure out what's going on," Heather told her, more as a warning than anything else. "I know if there was something you'd tell us, but seriously, what did you do?"

"I kind of want to know too," Robert chimed in. "Two of them cornered me the other day to ask. It was weird."

"I just asked them to find a guy my sister knew," Alice said, shrugging and keeping her eyes level with everyone else's. "They found some stuff about him, but they didn't like it."

"Was he into something?"

"Student Council?"

Robert laughed at that. "The way they were talking, I thought it was, like, the mafia or something."

The topic dropped from there, instead moving into dates for the end of the year dance. With only Heather having a date of the five of them, Robert offered to take Adrianna and Alice ended up with Kevin. Alice found herself actually looking forward to it, though there was something else she needed to do first.

It wasn't until they got back to the dorms that Alice managed to tell Adrianna about everything that happened, from the Bandersnatch to everything about Wonderland that she could manage. All the while, Alice went through the book, looking for anything she could on the Bandersnatch and how to make him give everyone back instead of just one person. Nothing. He traded wishes for sacrifices and never backed down on his word. If she wanted to release everyone, there was one thing she could do. A bet. It would be her life in exchange for the lives of the rest she was trying to free, though, and the Bandersnatch was very particular about following rules.

"So can you do the one thing?" Adrianna asked. "Maybe if you do a really good job keeping people away from him then he'll let you take more than just one person out of there. Maybe if you do a *really* good job, he'll let you take everyone."

"Maybe," Alice muttered, shutting the book. "I was trying to think of what to do with the Jubjub birds. I guess I could move them until they were all around the fog. Then people hear them and they'd stay away, right? You don't want to go into somewhere you can't see when you think someone might be getting murdered in there.

"I can help," Adrianna said. "The Jubjubs like me."

"It's too dangerous," Alice said. "And I don't want to drag you into this anymore. What if everyone forgot about you? Your brothers would be sad and they wouldn't even know why."

"You might disappear too, though," Adrianna said. "Then what?"

Alice didn't say anything, instead pulling her shoes back on. "I'm going to start digging holes. They like holes, right?"

Adrianna hesitated. "Maybe you could just study tonight. We do have finals coming up. If you fail those, you won't get to come back next year, right?"

Alice reluctantly took off her shoes and went back to her desk. Adrianna seemed relieved, but Alice frowned as she realized Adrianna was right. If she was going to go back to having a good life, she wanted it to be here and she needed to pass those finals. She could start working on the Jubjub birds after reading a few chapters.

As everyone fell into studying over the next few days, Alice joined them. The material wasn't too difficult, most of it things she had already learned before, and she felt confident about her chances to do well. With Robert determined to do well on his finals and Sarah no longer there to interrupt them with gossip, they spent most of their sessions focused, though Alice felt like something was missing.

At night, she would wait until Adrianna was asleep before slipping out. She found a shovel amidst the gardening supplies locked away in a shed on the school grounds and borrowed it. She spent an hour every night digging a long, narrow trench where the fog was only just beginning.

She would be back soon enough and quietly clean up, though she never felt rested the next morning. As the days passed, she grew more and more tired, though everyone else seemed too wrapped up in their studies to notice. Alice continued the motions, looking through the material and absorbing as much as she could.

The hardest part about exams was staying awake during them. Alice was exhausted by the last one, but continued to try and play the part of the good student and friend. She tried not to think of the trench in the woods, now large enough to try and get all the birds to go into it. She was almost finished.

"*Done!*" Robert said as they walked out of their last exam, stretching out his back and smiling widely. "Is it bad that I don't even care if I failed?"

"You didn't fail," Kevin told him.

"I need to go do something," Alice said and she started to walk away.

Heather grabbed her by the arm and pulled her back. "Unless that thing is sleep, no you don't," she told her. "Come on, celebration lunch and then we see if we can get one of the theatre rooms to watch *Lord of the Rings* until our brains melt."

"You really think she's going to make it to lunch?" Kevin asked. "No offense, but you look like you're going to fall over."

"I'm fine."

"You're really not. Don't worry," he said, looking at Heather, "We'll save the fun stuff for tomorrow."

"I'll help her back," Adrianna said. "I'll meet up with you guys in a bit."

"Do I really look that bad?" Alice asked as they walked off.

"You kinda do," Adrianna said. "Sorry. You probably just need some sleep though, right? You're just tired because you've been going out late every night."

Alice looked over to her. Of course she figured it out. "It's almost done, though. I just have a couple last things and then I don't have to do that anymore."

"You mean the thing with the Jubjubs?" Adrianna asked.

Alice nodded.

"Tonight, then," Adrianna said. "I can help you get them where you need them. They like me."

Alice nodded again. Now that they mentioned it, she was really tired.

"Until then, you should probably get some sleep." Adrianna opened the door to their room and let her in. Alice made a sound of approval and fell onto her bed, finding it entirely too comfortable to leave. She needed to move the Jubjub birds into the trench and convince the Bandersnatch to let both Evan and Sarah go, but for now her blankets had taken her.

When she woke up, the late afternoon light streamed through the window. Adrianna still wasn't back and Alice checked her clock to see that it was several hours later. With everyone still busy celebrating the completion of exams and Alice rested, she stepped off the bed and onto the forest floor.

CHAPTER 20

Done Deal

THERE WAS ONE particular Jubjub bird that was anxious to take a bite out of Alice whenever she got too close, so Alice used her hand as bait to lure it into the trench. It hobbled across the forest floor after her hand until it dropped into the hole in the ground. At first, it looked around and paced back and forth along the narrow opening. Once it found a spot it liked, it fluffed up its feathers and settled down in place.

The rest were more difficult. None of them found Alice's hands particularly tasty looking, so she needed to try something else. They wouldn't follow the tree branches she offered them and were not entranced by her attempts at singing, so she resorted to the one thing she knew worked on the Jabberwocky.

"*Ábedecian swég angrisla wudufugol hércyme!*" she shouted

into the woods. The Jubjub bird in the trench looked at her like she was a very tasty tree branch.

Alice almost wished Adrianna was here to help her lure the birds over. They followed her much more easily than they followed Alice, but she didn't want to risk her stumbling through the fog and encountering the Bandersnatch. Evan and Sarah were enough to worry about already.

The birds came in a stampede, stumbling over one another and their own feet as they wobbled forward, their bodies bobbing and their heads flopping about as they moved. Each fell into the trench, looking surprised and walking over one another to figure out their spots. Once each of them had fluffed out and settled down into the trench, they looked content.

"You're about to do something stupid again, aren't you?"

Alice looked and saw a splash of purple underneath the dirt of her shovel. She picked it up. It was almost over. She'd go in and fill her side of the deal before going back to school and forgetting about this whole mess. Evan would be back. Sarah would be back. Everyone else would return and it would be like nothing ever happened. She could have a normal school life and Wonderland would finally be behind her. This would be the last time she talked to Cat.

"I'm going to get everyone back," Alice told him.

"You've planted birds," Cat said. "If they become trees,

I would be quite upset if you did not permit me a sample of their fruit."

"What do you want?"

"Oh, why must you always assume that I want something?" he asked. "You know what is said about assumptions."

"You never want to just talk. Spit it out and let me get back to this. I'm almost done."

"Oh? Done?"

"The Jubjub birds will keep the unworthy away from the Bandersnatch. And with that settled, he owes me. If I threaten to take the birds away again, then he'll give me everyone else. I have it all figured out."

"So sure of yourself when you're being rude," Cat said. "Have we taught you nothing? Rudeness will get you nowhere in Wonderland or anywhere else, Alice."

"And what do you suggest?"

"I could give you a few ideas," Cat said, smiling and tapping at the shovel. "I am much better at negotiating than you are, Alice. You could bring me with you. As my thanks, I will not even ask anything more of you once I am through."

Alice dropped the shovel and walked into the fog. Almost over.

The fog was thick and went deep, but Alice was soon on the other side. Annoyance from Cat and determination of this almost being over fuelled her and she felt confident. One conversation with an incredibly powerful being. It would be easier than convincing the doctors that she wasn't crazy. She could do this.

The fog parted as she entered the huge room, the Bandersnatch again not there but there was a new statue. It was another student from the high school, though Alice again didn't recognize him. How could so many people have gone missing on such a small campus and no one noticed, even if no one remembered? Did the empty dorms seem strange to no one?

She stared up at him, straining to try and remember who he once was. She didn't think she'd ever seen him before. She went carefully through the garden, trying to put a name to all of them. Sarah she remembered fine. She was going to set Alice up on a date in a year. She would actually go on it if she could get her back. And then there was Evan, who people now realized was missing. There was a boy from the dorms that was two years ahead of her who Alice had seen but never met. Another girl she didn't know. The teacher. She wondered how anyone could have let him go missing without leaving behind a trace. He was being paid. He had accounts.

The bear catcher looked even younger now.

"Admiring my garden?"

Alice jumped back and spun around, the four eyes set in inky blackness immediately behind her. There wasn't even a texture to his body. It wasn't furry or scaly or even smooth. It was just there, solid and yet always threatening to swallow Alice up. She stared back at him and tried to think of something to say.

"Hello," she managed to get out. "I did what you asked."

"I know," he said, sweeping away to his seat at the head of this space and growing to a much larger size than before. Alice felt compelled to follow, though her mind was screaming at her to stay where she was and closer to an exit or something reflective. It seemed that he learned something from the last time and Alice found herself sitting back in the fluffy chair in front of his throne. He looked like he curled up in it, though with his body shifting so often it was hard to tell, and his head rested so that he could keep a close eye on Alice.

"Before all that, you have me quite curious, Alice Liddell."

Alice tried to remember to breathe. She was here for a reason. She knew it. That reason escaped her for the moment. "Oh?" she asked.

"You escaped me," he said. "Truth be told, I had expected to keep you for quite a bit longer than that. Long enough to have a decent conversation. I suspect, however, that was probably the best time to end it."

Alice didn't say anything. Her plan was suddenly not looking so good. The way he flicked open a claw to pick at his teeth in a mouth that hadn't been there a moment ago left her shifting in her seat, wondering what he might have gotten stuck in there. His teeth weren't even used for eating.

"I'm sorry," she managed to say, though her voice waivered as she spoke. She knew she needed to show less fear than any at all, but those teeth were distracting her.

"I would like to know where you fell to," he said. Alice felt something happen to her mind when he spoke. The reasons not to tell him too much were vanishing and she couldn't think of any reason not to tell him the truth.

"Wonderland," she said. She at least knew enough to tell only the truth and absolutely nothing more. He was trying to get her to say more with his eyes as they bored into her, but she had played this game before. Terrified or no, she knew how to keep from telling someone too much.

"I haven't ever truly seen Wonderland," he said after a moment, wistful as he ripped his eyes away from hers and out to the garden. "I was trapped in a book, you see. I heard many things, but I came to hate it there. It smells horribly of madness, much like you do. I almost can't stand to have you here, but you are interesting, Alice Liddell. And you have done me a favour."

"I put the Jubjub birds around your fog," she said. "Their calls should scare off anyone who comes too close."

"Yes, all of the unworthy will turn back from that," he said. He was amused by this, toying with something in his mind as he looked at Alice. Now, he was like an over-sized wolf and Alice felt very much like a small rabbit he had caught. "The rumours of my presence will start soon, as they always do. You will hear it in your school. There is something in the forest that grants wishes. I will have visitors soon enough, I imagine. Ones who are willing to trade important people to me for their desires. People given up by their friends in exchange for power always taste so much better."

Alice tried to smile and found she couldn't. Sure, some people would be spared because they were afraid and would turn back, but now there was a devil to sell your soul to in the forest. One that took other people instead of anything of yours. She wasn't going to be free of this thing until she sent it away or put it back in the book.

"You won't be putting me back in that book, child," he said, all four of his eyes falling square on her. She could tell he was both smiling and warning her. "Nor will you be sending me away. Although, I think I will welcome you here for a visit whenever you so choose. You are quite the curiosity."

"Thank you?"

"It is not a compliment," he said. "You smell of that wretched place, but you have the sense to be quiet now and then. Make no mistake, I know precisely what you are and what your task is. I want to see what Wonderland's hero will be doing in the coming days, now that one has been chosen. I daresay it will be the most fun I've had in years."

"I don't know what any of that means."

"You will, Alice Liddell. You will."

A chill went up Alice's spine at that. It sounded like this wasn't going to be over any time soon. It sounded like she was going to be dealing with this, and the Bandersnatch, for a while.

"Can you tell me now?" Alice asked hesitantly. "Please?"

The Bandersnatch let out a laugh, which did nothing to calm her nerves. She tried to focus on something else to calm down, but all she could think of were the other things he'd said. People were going to hear about him and start coming, willingly giving up their friends to make deals and no one would ever know.

"You can't do this," she said. "You can't just keep taking people."

"I won't be taking them, Alice Liddell," he said almost soothingly. "They will be given to me. An important distinction."

"You sound like the Cheshire Cat," Alice told him, sounding displeased and almost spitting out his name.

"Do I now?"

"At least I can make him stay in Wonderland. You are a different matter altogether."

"Comparing me to a pitiful creature from Wonderland and threatening to send me back to that wretched place is not the way to make me an ally, child. And I assure you, you do not want to make me an enemy."

Alice believed him, but the words were strange for her. "But you're from Wonderland."

Amusement flickered over him again. It was the dangerous sort and Alice had to back up as he leaned in to sneer at her. "And how did you come to that conclusion?"

Alice didn't want to answer, not sure what she was going to say that would offend the creature. Somehow, she couldn't keep herself from talking.

"You came out of the book and the book came from Wonderland."

"There is nothing about that book that implies that it is from Wonderland. There may be a madness about it, but it is nothing like yours, Alice Liddell. Surely you have noticed that much. There is much more at work here than you seem to realize."

"Will any of those things convince you to let all of these people go?"

When he let out a genuine laugh, the Bandersnatch was terrifying. "I usually detest heroes, but you amuse me, Alice Liddell. Not material to save anyone, unfortunately, but you should make this game interesting."

"I'm going to save at least them."

The Bandersnatch was still amused by her. "You'd leave everyone here if you could just bring those two back with you," the Bandersnatch said, looking at Evan and Sarah as statues in his garden. "No need to pretend otherwise."

"What do I need to do to get everyone else out of here?" Alice asked. "If I can convince you to leave, then will you give everyone back?"

"Now that sounds like an interesting wager," the Bandersnatch said. "I do enjoy a good bet. If you can get rid of me somehow, then I will gladly return everything I have taken in my time here." He slipped around to Alice's side, who was panicking. She did not know what was going on and the Bandersnatch stayed so close to her. "But conditions must apply, of course. It will need to be you, specifically, Alice Liddell, to get rid of me. No letting someone else get that honour. And a time limit is fair, I think. This seems like a fantastic challenge to have a hero try while the games are continuing out there. I propose by the time your tenure at that middle school ends. Do you agree?"

Alice absorbed the information and hesitated as she went over it all in her mind again. "Wait, slow down," she said, trying to get it all straight. "So you'll let all of them go if I can make you leave, right? And I have all the way until the end of middle school?"

"That's about right," he said, his voice curling into a sneer where his mouth did not. "You sound confident. Is it a bet?"

"It's a bet," Alice said. It would be easy. She had the brown book and in there, there were words she could use to tame the Jabberwocky and the Jubjub birds. There was probably something in there for even the Bandersnatch. The time limit would be of no consequence. It wouldn't take her that long to learn the spells she needed to lock him away somewhere else forever.

"I do hope you rely on that book of yours," the Bandersnatch said, slipping out into the garden of people. Alice felt the need to get up and follow him. "Frustrating though it might be, I have learned since it trapped me the last time. I would like to test myself."

Alice felt her hopes fall. She hoped he was lying, but she wasn't sure. She felt his power while in his presence, a cool and calm one that was contained and very well controlled. It was one that could make people disappear along with any memories of them. She wondered if it was even difficult for him.

"But there is another task at hand, dear, and you best complete it before you begin to bore me. While I may not harm you as Wonderland's hero, the longer you remain the more I feel the need to make your life more interesting to watch."

"Wait," Alice said, a thought occurring to her. "What if I don't make you leave? What happens then?"

"Why, the same thing that happens to everyone who loses a bet to me," he said, looking to one of the empty pedestals. This one was in gold and, when she looked directly at it, there was a golden statue of herself standing there. "I imagine with a few extra years on you, you will be delicious."

Alice needed to get everyone out of here now. Or, at least, the two she could. If the book didn't work, she would need to do something else. She didn't know what else, but something. Anything to not get unwritten.

She looked between Evan and Sarah, desperately trying to come up with a way to take them both when she watched the silver start to melt off of them. They were beginning to come around and Alice turned back to the Bandersnatch.

"Now, which of the two will you take in return for your good work?" the Bandersnatch asked. "Remember, you only get one."

"I want to save them both."

"Alice?"

Alice looked over at Sarah, who was looking around and scared. She came down off the pedestal and started walking over. The Bandersnatch wasn't there anymore, having melted away to let her decide for herself. "Alice where is this? I was just coming back with Robert and he thought he saw the ghost and started chasing after it and… and why are these statues all in silver? It's kind of tacky."

"I'm not sure I'd say tacky," Evan said, coming over to join them. "I'm more curious about where we are. And why Alex from fifth period is a statue."

"Well, Alice? Which one would you like to keep?"

"Alice?" Both eyes were on her and Alice shrunk under them. They wanted to know what was going on, but she couldn't tell them. It was her fault that one of them was going to be left behind. Unless she could think of something fast to make him let her keep them both.

"Both of them!" Alice yelled. "I want them both!"

"You don't get both," he said, Evan and Sarah looking around for the voice and where it was coming from. "One favour, one ornament from my garden. That is the deal."

"But that's not fair!" She felt Evan's hand on her shoulder trying to warn her not to argue, but she didn't listen to him.

"It's not. For me. It was such a small favour that I shouldn't even be giving you one."

"If it's so small, then maybe I should take the birds away!" Alice yelled at him. "Then anyone could walk in here and it would all taste terrible!"

"Alice!" Beside her, Sarah let out the one last cry before turning back to silver, frozen in place and looking desperately at Alice. Evan let out a strangled gasp as he watched at her, looking around with new eyes at all the statues around him and then back at Alice. Then at something else.

The Bandersnatch rose out of the ground in front of her, all four horrible eyes boring into her. "Your choice has been made. That one had a bit of an odd taste to him anyway."

"You can't!" Alice said, taking a step forward to him.

His patience was clearly wearing thin. "You will find I can do whatever I like. Do not forget our bet." He rose a hand and flicked his wrist.

ALICE SLAMMED HARD against a wall and collapsed onto a bookshelf below her. She let out a groan of pain and curled up, not sure what to do about anything now that everything hurt. She couldn't breathe and she wasn't sure if she was going to be able to stand for a while. She hit her head and the world spun around her. She thought she could hear someone calling her name.

"Did you see that?"

"I don't even know. She okay?"

"Hey Alice?"

Alice looked up, her head still spinning to see two of Adrianna's brothers bending over her. She couldn't tell who they were but she managed to let out a groan before letting her head rest back down on the ground again. Her head was still spinning.

There was a clunk behind them that distracted both of them. They perked up, looking back and Alice saw a new set of legs in the room. Evan's voice. He was back, thankfully, though the other two stayed back and shuffled around Alice with their hands up.

"She was like this when we got here," one said.

"We were just passing by."

"Forgot our books, you know. Exams and all."

"We weren't doing anything."

Alice couldn't keep track of it, their words coming out on top of one another instead of next to each other and they were desperately scrambling for excuses. It was going to take them a minute, Alice remembered. Like it took a minute for Adrianna.

"Have you guys gotten taller?" Evan demanded looking at them. "Lance, what's the date?"

"Hey! School!" one of them snapped. "How the hell did you know that?"

"Not right now," Evan said. "You would not believe the last five minutes I have had. Now, what's the date?"

"May 29th."

Evan hesitated. "What?"

"He said May 29th," Alice repeated, groaning as she tried to sit up. Everything she did hurt, but she managed to lean back against the bookshelf. "You've been gone a while."

"Alice, who is this guy?"

"Give it a minute," she said. "It'll come to you."

Evan was in front of her, checking to make sure she was okay. Her head felt like it was stuffed full of cotton, but everything started to clear up. Air filled her lungs and, with some help, she was able to get back up to her feet again.

"Why did you call him Lance?" Alice asked, looking around for someone else in the room in case she just missed something.

"Because no matter how much they like to make it as confusing for people as possible, their names are still Lance and Adam," Evan said, looking squarely over at the two of them.

"Except while we're at school," one of them said, sounding irritated. "That was the deal. How bad could your last five minutes have possibly been?"

Evan made a gesture at Alice.

"Mine were worse," Alice said. "Trust me." She couldn't meet any of their eyes.

"They're unfortunately about to get worse," a woman in the doorway said, turning on the lights to the classroom. "Out of bed after curfew *and* breaking into a classroom. You're all in a lot of trouble."

CHAPTER 21

The Cat Returns

"I CAN'T BELIEVE you have detention with my date," Heather said as she finished getting ready for the dance. Alice helped Adrianna and Heather get ready, Kevin offering to take Heather in Mark's place since Alice would not make it. Heather still seemed to be in good spirits about the whole thing; more curious about what Alice was doing out with them in the first place.

"I'm sorry," Alice said. Her shoulder still hurt and it was awkward for her to help, but she did her best. She was no Sarah when it came to it, but Heather knew how to make herself look good as it was.

"You have to find out what they were planning," Heather told her. "They were probably planning something big if they needed a third set of hands."

"Maybe they'll invite you along next time."

"There's a reason they asked you, Alice," Heather said, laughing. "You don't ask enough questions."

Alice saw them both off and went to her punishment. It was across campus in one of the studios. While Evan wasn't on his best form, he did manage to whittle down their punishment to just cleaning the studios and a call home. It took the woman a moment to remember Evan as well, and she was grateful to Mike and Mark — or Lance and Adam — that they were so willing to say they were at fault for Alice being there. They claimed that they brought her along as a punishment for catching them out of bed after hours.

Matt was there with them when Alice showed up, the cleaning woman handing them the materials and turning to Alice to give her the instructions. She seemed like a nice enough woman, more than happy to have the extra hands instead of having to do it all herself. She was especially friendly with the triplets, who were good workers and went right into cleaning without a second thought.

"They're good boys," she told Alice after giving her a rundown of the studio cleaning. "They pull jokes, but they always clean them up with no complaining. And their jokes are always so easy to clean up. Sometimes they help even when they are not caught. Good boys."

Alice smiled at that and got down to work with the rest

of them. The woman, Meredith, cleaned the washrooms while they worked on the front of the studio, leaving the music on so that they weren't bored and they could still have some fun, even if they were missing the dance with their friends.

"Can I trust you to do the rest?" Meredith asked.

"Yep!" the three boys said.

"I'll be back in one hour to lock up. If you finish early, you can go. See if you can make that dance of yours before it's over."

"Thank you, Meredith!"

Meredith laughed and waved as she left, leaving Alice with Matt, Mark and Mike to clean the main body of the studio. They needed to clean the floor as well as polish the mirrors before they could leave, though they waited only until they started working before they started talking to one another.

"So did you guys actually manage to pull off anything?" Matt asked, joining Alice in sweeping the floor while the other two started working on getting the mops ready and the things to wash the mirrors.

"Yeah, we were done before we got caught," Mark said. "They aren't even going to know until next year. It's going to be great."

"What did you do?" Alice asked.

"Covered the white boards," Matt said. "Clear coat over the top of it makes it impossible to write on. Should keep the first day back exciting."

"Why would you even want to do that?" Alice asked, leaning on her broom as they finished the sweep. Mark and Mike were already ready with the mops and started working on the floors before Alice had finished sweeping. Matt went to the mirrors, waving Alice away given her shoulder and she took a seat against the far wall to watch as they did the rest.

"Because it's funny?" Matt said. "Classes are the most boring part of school, so why not make them a little more interesting, you know?"

"But you're supposed to be here to get a good education, aren't you?"

"No," Mark said. "We're here to have good *life* experiences. We have brothers to be successful for us. We're thinking about going off and doing something a little different. Don't know what, yet. Maybe hacking into governments and holding things for ransom until we get caught."

"Evan should be president by that time, so he'll get us off easy," Matt said with a bit of a wink.

"Or we'll piss him off and we'll get the death penalty," Mike said, turning to Alice. "Speaking of Evan, though. There's the matter of how you got us to look up all that stuff on our own brother earlier this semester. I don't know what happened there. I have emails asking my brothers who the hell this guy is and them replying that they have no idea. I don't even remember why we were looking him up in the first place, but I remember it had something to do with you."

"Are you sure?" Alice asked, keeping her face neutral and meeting his eyes.

"Oh, I'm sure," Mark said. "I remember looking through all those old sites because Alice was on to something about this guy."

"It's not like he was even gone," Matt chimed in. "Evan's been here all semester."

"I don't know," Alice said.

All three of them studied her and she kept her expression blank, meeting their eyes until they backed off.

"There's something weird about you," Mark said, Alice keeping herself relaxed, though inside she started to go through a list of things to say. Weird was a bad word. It was one of those words that might land her back in a hospital or on a prescription if she wasn't careful. "First you got us to look up our brother, then you vanish out of our third floor dorm room and end up unconscious in the forest outside school bounds. And then I swear you showed up out of thin air in the class-room to get us all caught."

"I'm pretty sure she disappeared a few times when she was walking with Addie too," Matt said. "One minute she's there, the next, vanished."

"Yeah, I noticed that too," Mike said. "What's going on, Alice? What aren't you telling us?"

"It's probably just your imagination," Alice said. She'd been here before. She knew how to handle this. "Think about it. How could anyone do anything you just said? People don't appear out of thin air and they don't disappear either. You probably were just seeing things."

"Then why was Evan saying you would know about his crazy five minutes?"

"I think the better question is why you guys didn't recognize him when he showed up," Alice said. "What was all that about how you just found me like that and how you could explain?"

"Well, it was pretty suspicious," Mike said.

"I'm sure it was, *Lance*," she said, glaring at him and crossing her arms.

"She found out about the name thing?" Matt asked, looking disappointedly at his brothers.

"Evan told her," Mark said. "We have to explain it now, don't we?"

"What's to explain?" Matt asked. "It's easier for people to

mix us up if we have similar names, so they used their middle names. Easy."

"And then it's harder for people to figure out who did what and then we can pull the wrongfully accused card and *usually* we can get off completely."

"She's got us off topic," Mike said, bringing them back together.

Alice came forward and helped them get cleaning supplies, the room so clean now that it glistened. They let her sit back down on the floor as they moved everything out of the room to where Meredith could pick it up. When they returned, they shut the door behind them and took a seat in a row against the mirrors in front of Alice, Matt sticking his leg out to block the door.

"We just want to talk. Pray tell, Alice," Mark said. "How did you get out and back into the dance last time?"

"I..." Alice began, debating whether she wanted to join them or not. She looked them over, trying to determine whether or not this was some sort of trick.

Something appeared above their heads in the mirror. A purple blob was watching, the mirror around him shifting as he did so. It was like Wonderland was moving around him.

Alice tore her eyes away from the sight and looked back down at Adrianna's brothers. The only time Cat ever spoke in front of anyone other than Alice, it was Adrianna. He hadn't even spoken when her mother was around. Cat wouldn't do anything, not now.

"I walked," she said firmly.

"In the snow. In girly shoes."

"I may have also done some running," Alice said.

"Running that left no footprints."

"I...."

Above them the Cheshire Cat opened his eyes and a wide, toothy grin appeared in the purple mess of fur.

"Have you been seeing another cat, Alice?" the mocking voice of Cat said. "Something has clearly caught your tongue and I don't appear to have it here. Or have you forgotten that night so completely?"

Her heart leapt into her throat. He wasn't supposed to talk to her now — not with other people just on the other side of the mirror. She wouldn't be able to explain away a talking purple cat in the mirror.

She watched helplessly as Cat stepped out of the mirror beside Adrianna's brothers, Wonderland shifting and changing behind him as he became human once more. Alice scrambled backwards, trying to get to her feet while the boys turned to watch him, Cat ignoring their eyes.

"But you said you couldn't get out," Alice said, trying

to understand what was happening. "You're not supposed to get out!"

"Weren't you kicked out or something?" Matt asked, starting to get to his feet.

"Dude, he just walked through the mirror," Mark hissed at him, pulling him back.

"That's not possible," Mike said.

"It's as if you aren't happy to see me, Alice. Perhaps there's too much to pay attention to in here."

Cat turned back to Mike, Mark and, Matt. The three of them scrambled to their feet, using the mirror to balance. The mirror shifted and their hands fell through the glass, followed by the rest of them.

Alice jumped forward and hit the glass when she tried to grab them. She didn't understand it. Wonderland was right there. She could do it before, so why was it not working now? She pounded on the glass, desperately trying to get back through, but Wonderland shifted again and again under her fingertips.

"Still won't listen to me?" Cat said. "You have yet to learn any manners, have you?"

"What did you do?" Alice demanded, rounding on him. Her face felt wet. "Bring them back!"

"I don't think I will," he said. "Not when you ask in such a manner. If you didn't want to talk to me, Alice, just say so."

"You can't just throw people into Wonderland! Let me in! I need to get them back!"

"Have a wonderful summer, Alice," Cat said, vanishing. "It might be a little busy."

About the Author

TANYA LISLE IS a novelist from Metro Vancouver, British Columbia, who has series littered across genres from supernatural horror to young adult fantasy. She began writing in elementary school, when she started turning homework assignments into short stories and continued this trend well into university. While attending Simon Fraser University, she developed an appreciation for public domain crossovers and cross-platform narratives. She has a shelf full of notebooks with more story ideas than pens lost to the depths of her bag. Now she writes incessantly in hopes of finishing all of them.

Thankfully, her cat, Remy, has figured out how to shut off Tanya's computer when she needs to take a break.